THE
STORIES
HE
TOLD

THE STORIES HE TOLD

The Dubno Maggid
on the
Weekly Parashah

Volume 1
Bereishis - Vayikra

Miriam Rosenzweig

TARGUM/FELDHEIM

First published 1991

Copyright © 1991 by M. Rosenzweig

ISBN: 0-944070-70-1 hardcover
ISBN: 0-944070-71-X paperback

Phototypeset at Targum Press

Published by:
Targum Press Inc.
22700 W. Eleven Mile Rd.
Southfield, Mich. 48034

Distributed by:
Feldheim Publishers
200 Airport Executive Park
Spring Valley, N.Y. 10977

Distributed in Israel by:
Nof Books Ltd.
POB 23646
Jerusalem 91235

Printed in Israel

בס"ד

מוקדש בהערצה לזכרו של
אבי מורי

יעקב בן אברהם צבי ע"ה

אשר דמותו נצבת חיה לנגד עינינו
כדוגמה להצנע לכת, כבוד הבריות,
ואהבת ישראל פעילה ומסורה.

נלב"ע י"ד סיון תשי"ז

ת.נ.צ.ב.ה.

This book is dedicated to the cherished memory
of my late father,
Yaakov ben Avrohom Tsvi Kokis,
whose sterling qualities of humility
and untiring devotion to the welfare
of one's fellow Jew
serve as an example to his children
and grandchildren yet today.

Contents

Introduction

This is a book of *meshalim* (parables) first told by the Dubno Maggid about two hundred years ago.

A *mashal* is a story, but it is more, too. A good *mashal* is like a mirror: it gives us information about ourselves. A *maggid* holds a mirror/*mashal* up to us to tell us something we don't usually notice. For instance, I can look at my feet and see whether my shoes need polishing. But when it comes to my face, I can't be sure I've wiped away that last smudge of chocolate milk until I take a good look in the mirror.

In Hebrew, the words *panim* (face) and *penim* (inner being) are closely related. (Doesn't the expression on our *face* reveal what we feel *inside*?) Just as a mirror can help us see our own faces, so a *mashal* can clarify what is happening in our hearts. We read about the proud prince or the rebellious son, and laugh, cry, or worry with him. Then, when the story comes to an end, the *maggid* points a finger at the characters he has created and tells us, "Look again. Look closely at Chaim or Ronald." We peer intently at the *maggid*'s heroes, and lo and behold, the king's arrogant daughter and the tailor's wayward son are none other than ourselves! Having enjoyed a pleasant tale, often with a clever, surprise ending, we have learned something new about ourselves. And had a good time, too!

Not every *mashal* tells us about ourselves personally. Some explain how Hashem rules the world, how we should understand a seemingly difficult *pasuk*, or how to view the role of *Am Yisrael* in Hashem's plan for the whole world. Each *mashal* has its own message, its own lesson to enrich our lives.

Over four hundred of the Dubno Maggid's *meshalim* were recorded and published in Hebrew after his death. Only a portion of them could be included in this collection, but hopefully, they will whet your appetite for more.

The Maggid's full name was Rabbi Yaakov ben Ze'ev (Wolf) Kranz. He was born in 1741 in the town of Zeitil, near Vilna, where his father served as the Rav of the Jewish community. He studied at home with his learned father until the age of eighteen, when he left to study in Mezritch. There he began his career as a *maggid*, a public speaker and teacher. Later, Rabbi Kranz moved on to other locations, but it was in the town of Dubno (where he remained for eighteen years) that he gained fame and became known as the Dubno Maggid.

Public speaking was only one facet of the Maggid's active life. He was also a brilliant and diligent Gemara scholar, remaining in the *beis midrash* each morning after Shacharis and learning until noon, when he would have his first meal of the day.

The Maggid's afternoons were devoted to teaching yeshivah students. Here again, the *mashal* was a favorite tool of instruction in explaining the Torah and Midrash.

In addition, the Maggid was very much in touch with the day-to-day lives of his congregants and fellow Jews. He had the *shamash* of the synagogue quietly report to him when illness or tragedy struck members of the community. Each day he would tearfully recite a few chapters of Tehillim on their behalf.

The Maggid also traveled throughout Poland and Germany, helping his fellow Jews improve their Torah observance.

In the course of his travels, he befriended the renowned Vilna Gaon, Rabbi Eliyahu (1720-

1797), and became a staunch admirer of his teachings. It is said that during his later years, when the Gaon sometimes felt too weak to learn with his usual intensity, he would ask the Maggid to share some of his artful *meshalim* and Torah insights. The two men respected each other highly, and after the Gaon's passing, the Maggid skillfully invented *meshalim* to explain his late friend and teacher's lofty ideas to the common Jew.

The Maggid himself passed away seven years later, in 1804, in the town of Zamosc. Only then were his teachings committed to writing and eventually published, thanks to his only son, Rav Yitzchak, and Rabbi Avraham Dov Berish Flahm, who had not known the Maggid but felt very devoted to his memory and his teachings. These two men collected the Maggid's notes, recorded his interpretations, and published several volumes of his works:

- *Ohel Yaakov* — a four-volume commentary on *Chumash*
- *Kol Yaakov* — on the Five Megillos (Shir HaShirim, Rus, Eichah, Koheles, and Esther)
- *Kochav MiYaakov* — on the haftorahs
- *Emes LeYaakov* — on the Hagaddah
- *Sefer HaMiddos* — essays on *yiras shamayim*, *ahavas Hashem*, and *tefillah*

The Maggid's special tool, the *mashal,* appears again and again throughout his works. Even difficult concepts, such as the command to rise above the influence of the constellations, become clear when explained by the Maggid's parables.

Many of the *meshalim* retold here were originally much shorter, while the lessons they teach were often accompanied by more involved discussions and by references to additional verses in the Torah and Midrash. Although the Maggid's stories are highly entertaining, he was far from a mere writer of tales for children. All agree that his narratives are lucid and appealing even on their own, but he composed them not for their own sake, but to drive home a spiritual lesson, and often a sophisticated one at that.

The Jewish people has known a myriad of brilliant scholars such as the Maggid, but few, if any, have ever matched his exceptional ability to find in everyday life perfect illustrations of ideas expressed in the Tanach. The Maggid's tales thus served as a bridge enabling even the simple or untutored to cross over the moat of ignorance that separated him from the King's wondrous palace of Torah knowledge and the treasures stored therein.

It is the author's hope and prayer that the *meshalim* in this book will likewise afford Jews of all ages and backgrounds a glimpse of Hashem's infinite treasure trove of exquisite gems, enhancing their appreciation of the priceless Torah heritage He has bequeathed to His people Israel.

The author wishes to thank Rabbi Yonasan Rosenblum, editor of the English-language edition of *Yated Ne'eman*, who reviewed the material in this book and offered helpful suggestions; and the entire staff of Targum Press, whose patience and encouragement smoothed many a wrinkle as this book came into being.

Bereishis

A Blessing or a Curse?

...אֲרוּרָה הָאֲדָמָה בַּעֲבוּרֶךָ בְּעִצָּבוֹן תֹּאכְלֶנָּה כֹּל יְמֵי חַיֶּיךָ.
וְקוֹץ וְדַרְדַּר תַּצְמִיחַ לָךְ וְאָכַלְתָּ אֶת עֵשֶׂב הַשָּׂדֶה.

*...the ground is cursed for your sake; you shall
eat of it in sadness all the days of your life. It
will grow thorns and thistles for you, and you
will eat the grass of the field.*

(Bereishis 3:17-18)

FTER ADAM HARISHON ate from the *eitz
hada'as* (tree of knowledge), Hashem told
him that from now on he would have to
work very hard to grow his own food. It is clear
why Adam was punished, but why did Hashem
use the expression "for your sake," as though
cursing the ground and making life harder for
Adam were a favor to him?

The Dubno Maggid explains with a *mashal*:

Lord Harris was one of the wealthiest landowners in the entire country. Often his friends would ask him how he managed a large farm, many quarries, and extensive forestlands all at the same time. The answer was always the same:

"Thanks to my faithful, talented manager, Stanley. I could never do it without him. He knows just when to buy and when to sell; whom to trust with credit and whom to refuse; how many acres to sow with wheat and how many with oats; which cows produced the most milk last year, and which hens the most eggs."

In contrast, Henry, Lord Harris's only son, had no idea whatsoever about his father's business dealings. Henry knew how to ride horses; he played several instruments well, spoke a passable French, and was very much at home when discussing the most popular authors and their latest books. But of crops and trees, sheep and cattle, and mines and quarries, he knew nothing at all. Lord Harris doted on his only child and had never wanted to trouble him with the burdens of running a huge estate.

"Let him enjoy himself while he is young," Lord Harris would say.

"Yes, there's no need to trouble him with

thoughts of profits and losses and loans and interest for now," Lady Harris agreed. "There will be enough time for all that when we are old and gray and cannot manage without his help."

Stanley, however, felt otherwise. He resented the way Lord Harris sheltered Henry, but of course it was not his place to say anything to either one. He continued to serve Lord Harris as faithfully as ever, but he found a way to let out his resentment:

Whenever Stanley had to travel into one of the nearby villages to buy something or hire crafts-men, he would invite Henry along. Stanley always spoke in a fatherly voice and promised to show the boy interesting sights on the way. Lord Harris was pleased that his manager showed such warmth and concern for his Henry, and readily agreed to let him accompany Stanley on such trips. No one suspected that he really disliked the boy intensely.

Once they were on the road, Stanley would tell the lad frightening stories of ghosts and goblins and demons — things that never existed — and of terrifying events that never happened. Henry knew that his father trusted his manager com-pletely, and he believed every word he heard. The boy's eyes would grow wide with a mixture of terror and fascination, and Stanley would silently gloat over how naive and foolish was this pampered, overprotected lad who would one day inherit all his master's wealth.

When they arrived in the village, Henry would marvel at all the sights, but Stanley had no patience for his questions and comments. The way home would be spent silently looking out the window, and by the time they returned to the castle, it would seem that Henry had completely forgotten Stanley's tales of terror.

But all was not well. Henry did not forget entirely. He began to wake up at night quaking with fear and bathed in sweat. Stanley's stories played on his mind and the boy would relive them, actually seeing horrid creatures chasing after him. Then he would scream so loud that he'd wake himself up — and half the castle as well. His parents would come running to his bedside and try to calm him, but most nights he could not fall asleep again.

Lord and Lady Harris could not understand why their precious son should suddenly start suffering from nightmares. They changed his diet, gave him a softer mattress, and even changed his bedroom so that he would have less of a draft at night.

But nothing helped. Henry continued to wake up screaming dreadfully night after night.

"Let's ask Dr. Navonman," pleaded Lady Harris in despair. "He's always been so helpful and caring toward Henry."

Lord Harris agreed, and the doctor was summoned. He carefully examined the patient and found him hale and hearty, apart from a lack of sleep. Then he started inquiring into the nature of Henry's dreams. As the boy answered the doctor's questions and started to describe the monsters and demons that haunted his mind each night, his face clearly showed the fears that tormented him. Dr. Navonman was perturbed.

"Where did you read such rubbish about demons and devils and the like?" he exclaimed.

"I didn't read it, sir," Henry explained. "Stanley told me all about them. He knows. He's seen them himself."

"Stanley? Seen demons and dragons? Ridiculous! Poppycock! Stanley's seen as many demons as he has pink horses. When did he tell you such drivel? And why should you believe him?"

Henry explained everything. He told the doctor and his parents about his trips with Stanley and the fascinating — but terrifying — stories the manager always had for him.

Lord Harris began to understand what had been happening during the past several weeks. But he was at a loss to help his son forget what he had heard and get over his deep fears. He sent

Henry off to play, and sat down with Lady Harris and the doctor to find a solution.

"What do you think, Doctor? Can we make him forget? Will he ever be able to sleep peacefully again?"

"I think we *can* help him to forget it all, and to sleep as well as ever. But we must fill his days to the brim with work, real work. Not flute-playing or horseback-riding or other amusements.

"Lord Harris, you must involve him in the management of your estate and see that his thoughts are occupied from dawn to dusk with things that really exist and really matter. Now he is too protected, too removed from real life. His mind is free to fantasize about things that exist only in his imagination — and Stanley's. But if you fill his head with very real concerns, there'll be no room left for the rubbish Stanley has been feeding him."

Lord Harris thanked the doctor and said good-bye. Then he immediately summoned Stanley.

"You have poisoned my son's mind with your evil stories of dragons and demons, and robbed us all of our sleep for weeks now. Your services are no longer required here, Stanley. Leave at once!"

"But...but, my lord!" stuttered Stanley, aghast at being fired. "I can understand you are annoyed

"You have poisoned my son's mind with your evil stories of dragons and demons.... Leave at once!"

that the stories have frightened my young master, but, all in all, have I committed so great a crime with a few amusing fairy tales that I should be punished so severely? I have a wife and children; where shall I take them? How shall I feed them? Surely I do not deserve so great a penalty as dismissal, my lord."

"I'm not firing you to punish you, Stanley. I'm firing you to cure my son. As long as you are here to manage everything, he will never become truly involved in the management of my estates. He will know that he can always rely on you to do whatever he leaves undone.

"But if I send you away, things will be different. When I give him a task to do, he will know that it is his responsibility, and his alone, to see that it gets done properly and promptly. That is just what he needs to be cured. And it won't happen until you leave. I'm sending you away not because I want to punish you, but because I want to cure Henry. You'll have to go!"

Chazal tell us: "Torah study is good when combined with an occupation, for the effort of both together makes one forget sin" (*Avos* 2:2).

The way to avoid sinning, Chazal teach us, is to keep busy all the time. When Adam and Chavah

were first created, they were served by the serpent, who met all their needs. There was no
reason to worry about growing crops or preparing
food; the serpent, who could walk upright and
speak, waited on them constantly. Adam and
Chavah were at leisure, so there was time for the
serpent to start a conversation with Chavah and
get her to sin — and to tempt Adam.

People who are busy have no time for *aveiros*.
After Adam sinned, Hashem gave him a way to
protect himself from transgressing again: "the
ground is cursed for your sake." "For your sake"
means "for your benefit." From now on, you will
have to plow the ground, plant seeds, tend crops,
harvest and thresh grain, grind wheat and mill it
into flour, mix dough, and bake it into bread.
Why? Because then you will be too busy to listen
to the evil inclination a second time. The earth's
curse was actually a blessing in disguise for
Adam, to help him avoid being tricked by the
nachash into disobeying Hashem's commandments in the future.

Even when Hashem punishes us, He does so
in a way that will help us do *teshuvah*, for, as
Chazal teach us, "Everything Hashem does, He
does only for good."

Noach

Choosing Wisely

וַיָּחֶל נֹחַ אִישׁ הָאֲדָמָה וַיִּטַּע כָּרֶם.

And Noach began to be a man of the earth, and he planted a vineyard.

(Bereishis 9:20)

AFTER THE FLOOD, Hashem promised Noach and his family that He would never bring another flood on the world. So Noach started to grow crops again, first planting a vineyard.

Chazal tell us that Noach should have planted a different crop, not grapes. Why? Aren't grapes — and the wine they give us — important? We use wine for kiddush, and the *pasuk* tells us that "wine gladdens a man's heart" (Tehillim 104:15). Why was it a mistake for Noach to choose this as his first crop?

The Dubno Maggid explains with a *mashal.*

S ay, Simchah, isn't that the saintly Reb Meshulam sitting over there at the large, round table?"

"Where?" Simchah nearly jumped to his feet in excitement. "Here in the Royal Eagle Inn? Right here in the room with us?"

The two friends approached the kitchen, looking for the owner of the Royal Eagle, but they were nearly bowled over by a pair of waiters bearing heavy platters destined for the honored guest and his party.

David accosted one of them. "Tell me, isn't that Reb Meshulam the tzaddik sitting there at the main table in the dining room?"

"It sure is," answered one waiter tersely, "and I've got to get this platter over there quickly. Sorry..." he called breathlessly as he scurried after his friend.

"What good luck!" David exclaimed, hugging Simchah excitedly. "The tzaddik himself. Now all we have to do is wait patiently for the right moment and then ask for a *berachah.* Everyone knows that the tzaddik's *berachos* are fulfilled. Come, let's sit right here where we can see everything. When his *shamash* gets up, we'll ask him exactly what to do."

Two hours later, Simchah and David left the Royal Eagle smiling from ear to ear. "A *berachah* from the tzaddik!" David told everyone who would listen.

"Did you hear what he said to me?" Simchah asked his friend. "He said that I'd have fantastic success with the very first thing I do when I get home. You know what I'm going to do? I'm going to take out the purse of gold coins I have hidden away — all our savings — and I'm going to sit down and start counting it. I'm going to be rich, David, you hear? A millionaire! Imagine it...I can't wait!"

With these words, Simchah quickened his pace, pulling David along with him. Soon they reached the corner where their ways parted.

Simchah hardly paused to say goodbye to his friend, but David faithfully wished him good luck and called out as he waved, "Let me know what happens. *Be'ezras Hashem*, I'll help you celebrate your new wealth!"

"Good luck to you, too!" called Simchah as he disappeared down the lane. A minute later, he burst through his front door with the good news.

"Saraleh! Quick! I met the tzaddik! Bring me the purse with the gold coins! Right away!"

Poor Saraleh. Not even a "*shalom aleichem*" from her husband — or a word of explanation. All she could conclude was that Simchah had met some great rebbe who needed funds quickly, and that her good-hearted husband intended to give away a lifetime of savings. She had to know what was happening here — what was so urgent?

"First tell me what happened, Simchah. Then I'll get the purse. Just tell me what you're so excited about," requested Saraleh.

"No! No! Don't put it off. I need it right now, this minute! First thing! Where is it? Where did you put it?"

"Have a drink," Saraleh urged, trying to set out a cup and saucer for Simchah, but he wouldn't be put off.

"No! No! Stop playing foolish games! I don't need hot tea now. You'll ruin everything with your silly tea! The money! Bring me the money!" Simchah fumed.

But the more Simchah screamed and panicked, the more reluctant Saraleh became to hand over all their savings in the blink of an eye. "No, no. First let's discuss it."

The "discussion" grew into an argument, and the argument into a full-blown cat-and-dog fight. And who was the winner? Why, Simchah, of course. Hadn't the tzaddik promised him success in the first thing he did when he got home? The very first act...even if it was a tiff with his wife!

So Simchah won...and Simchah lost. He lost his chance to make the *berachah* count. Instead of a blessing of wealth, he was blessed with success in outscreaming his poor wife. A minor gain...and a major loss!

Even a *berachah* from Reb Meshulam himself couldn't save Simchah from his own lack of foresight.

"*Vayachel Noach*" (And Noach began) can also be read, "And Noach profaned" — he made himself *chol*, the opposite of *kadosh*, holy. The *Chumash* uses the word "*vayachel*," with its double meaning of "begin" and "profane," to teach us that Noach profaned himself when he chose grapes as the very first crop to raise on earth after everything had been destroyed.

Why? Because grapes give us wine, and wine can lead to serious mistakes and *aveiros*.

After the flood, Noach had been assured by Hashem that whatever he did to build the world anew would be blessed with success. But it was up to Noach to decide what to do with this blessing. Noach chose to plant a grapevine that he had taken into the ark with him.

The blessing took effect immediately. The same day that Noach planted his vineyard, the vines blossomed and produced fruit; that same day, Noach picked the grapes and made wine from them. And that same day, he became drunk — and disgraced himself.

Like Simchah in the Maggid's *mashal*, Noach had been promised a *berachah*. But a blessing carries with it a responsibility; it must be used with caution, like a powerful tool. Part of our job is to think ahead, to ask ourselves: What will be the results of my actions? Will they make Hashem happy? Will He be pleased with the way I used the blessing He gave me?

Noach's lack of forethought led to his own disgrace and a curse for Canaan, his grandson. Even today, thousands of years later, Canaan's descendants still live with the effects of that curse. Like Simchah in the *mashal*, even Noach — who was such a tzaddik that he was privileged to build the world afresh after the flood — even Noach lost out when he acted without thinking.

On the other hand, when we consider our actions carefully and act accordingly, the blessings we receive last for years and years afterwards. As the *pasuk* says: "The blessing of Hashem enriches and He will not add sorrow with it" (Mishlei 10:22).

Lech Lecha

It's Not in the Stars

וַיּוֹצֵא אֹתוֹ הַחוּצָה וַיֹּאמֶר הַבֶּט נָא הַשָּׁמַיְמָה וּסְפֹר הַכּוֹכָבִים
אִם תּוּכַל לִסְפֹּר אֹתָם וַיֹּאמֶר לוֹ כֹּה יִהְיֶה זַרְעֶךָ.

*And [Hashem] took him outside and said:
"Look now toward the heavens and count the
stars, if you can count them;" and He said to
him: "So [numerous] shall your offspring be."*
(Bereishis 15:5)

HASHEM PROMISED AVRAHAM that just
as the stars are too numerous to count,
so, too, would his offspring be so numerous that people would not be able to count them
all.

The Midrash tells us that Avraham was convinced he would never have children: he had seen
in the stars that he was fated to be childless. But

Hashem told him: "Give up your speculations about the stars saying you won't have a child in the future. *Avram* won't have a child, but *Avraham* will; *Sarai* will not give birth, but *Sarah* will. I will call you different names and your fortune will change."

According to the Midrash, Hashem also promised to show Avraham how the very same star that seemed to indicate a fate of childlessness now revealed that he would indeed have a son.

The Dubno Maggid asks how this could be: How could the same star indicate two opposite things: barrenness, on the one hand, and becoming the father of a whole nation, on the other?

The Maggid answers his question with a *mashal*:

There, that's the last one," declared Naftali with a smile of satisfaction as he tucked another carefully wrapped gold coin into its hiding place. "It's all away, safe and sound. You can sleep peacefully now: here in a big city like Grosstown, with a fine force of constables and a strict police chief like Herr Tokiff, you've got nothing to worry about. In Eckville there's nothing for a thief to be afraid of, but who would dare steal here in Grosstown?"

Eckville was little more than a crossroads

dotted by a few houses. By far the largest building in the tiny village was Shloimy's Silver Swan Inn. Over the years, he and his wife Raizy had built it up, adding more rooms and taking on additional staff until it had become a landmark on the road to Grosstown. Meanwhile, Shloimy had become a wealthy man, and had saved up a considerable sum for his daughter's wedding someday.

Shloimy and Raizy were uneasy about keeping so much money in the Silver Swan, where strangers came and went all the time. So they hit upon the plan of transferring their savings to Shloimy's brother Naftali's house in town. Naftali had only two servants, Johann and his wife, both of whom could be fully trusted. Thus, the day Shloimy returned home from Grosstown and reported that everything was safely hidden away in Naftali's house, Raizy breathed a sigh of relief.

Months passed, and life carried on as usual. Neither brother gave much thought to the treasure hidden away in Naftali's house. Then one autumn day, Naftali's servant Johann came galloping down the path to the Silver Swan. Even before he dismounted, he shouted out the bad news: "Thieves! It's gone! Robbers! Master Naftali said to tell you they took everything!"

Shloimy didn't waste a minute. Running to his stables, he barked orders to his men.

"Dietrich! Saddle up the four fastest steeds! You'll go northward with Johann and I'll take the southern road with Friedreich. They can't have gone far with all that weight to carry. Quickly! There's no time to lose!"

"But Master Shlomo!" Johann protested. "They've gone already! There's nothing we can do now — it's too late. Master Naftali said nothing about trying to catch the thieves. He told me to tell you what happened, but he said nothing about chasing after them. It's hopeless!"

"Don't be silly, Johann. Of course there's a chance we'll catch them. If my brother Naftali didn't think so, why would he have sent you galloping over here at top speed to tell me what happened? He wouldn't be in such a rush just to share some bad news with me.

"He must believe that there is still a chance to catch the robbers and get the money back. The very fact that you are standing here now is proof of that. Your words tell me one thing, but your presence here tells me just the opposite. So let's get going!"

Hashem has many messengers. Long ago, when there were prophets, Hashem sent messages with them, sometimes to individuals and sometimes to an entire nation. For example, on

Yom Kippur, we read how Hashem sent the prophet Yonah to Nineveh to warn the people that the whole city would be destroyed.

In the time of Avraham Avinu, before the days of the prophets, Hashem used other ways of giving messages, such as the star that "told" Avraham (in a way we no longer understand) he could not have children. But if he would "chase after" the *zechus* of having children, and pray to be granted a son worthy of carrying on his mission of teaching the world about Hashem, then he *would* be blessed with a child. Hashem sent the "messenger" to Avraham not because He sought to give him bad news, *chas vechalilah*, but because He wanted him to earn that son by praying for him.

How was Avraham Avinu to know that Hashem wanted him to pray? Only by seeing some sign that, as things stood right then, he still needed more meritorious deeds in order to earn the priceless privilege of becoming the father of Yitzchak Avinu. In this case, the messenger Hashem sent him was a star.

At first Avraham Avinu understood the star to mean that he would never have children, just as Johann thought the brothers would never get the stolen property back. He didn't realize that the whole point of his dash to the Silver Swan was to give Shloimy a chance to rescue his savings, not to tell him all was lost.

Similarly, Hashem told Avraham Avinu that the whole point of the star's message was for him to rise above the fate of childlessness by adding prayer after prayer to his merits until he became worthy of becoming the father of Yitzchak Avinu. If there had indeed been no hope of Avraham eventually being blessed with a son, there would have been no reason for Hashem to show him the star in the first place.

Once Avraham Avinu had seen the star's message, Hashem told him: "Give up your ideas about what the star says; rise above its message by gaining additional merits, for then you will be blessed with generation after generation of offspring as numerous as the stars, which cannot even be counted."

VaYeira

Merit Enough for All

וַה׳ אָמָר הַמְכַסֶּה אֲנִי מֵאַבְרָהָם אֲשֶׁר אֲנִי עֹשֶׂה. וְאַבְרָהָם
הָיוֹ יִהְיֶה לְגוֹי גָּדוֹל וְעָצוּם....

*And Hashem said: "Shall I hide from Avraham
what I am going to do, seeing that Avraham
will surely become a great and mighty nation...?"*

(Bereishis 18:17-18)

SEDOM AND AMORAH were large cities in Eretz
Yisrael, near the Dead Sea. The people living
there in the time of Avraham Avinu had been
wicked for many, many years. Not only did they
ignore Hashem's commandments, but they also
dealt cruelly with their fellow men. Hashem was
about to punish them by destroying their cities. But
first He decided to inform Avraham Avinu of His plan.

The *Chumash* tells us why: "Avraham will surely become a great and mighty nation."

This seems to be a strange reason for Hashem to let a person know what He is planning to do. What does Avraham's becoming a great nation in the future have to do with Hashem's punishment of two wicked cities right now?

The Dubno Maggid explains with a *mashal*:

Two merchants from Kranzville were in Leipzig for the fair: Reb Shlomo, who dealt in spices, and the much younger Reb David, who sold all kinds of housewares.

Since it was Reb David's first trip, Reb Shlomo, who had been to Leipzig more times than he could remember, was showing his young companion around the teeming marketplace. Past the food stalls, they came upon row after row of clothing shops. Here both men slowed their pace and looked with interest at the array of finely tailored suits and coats on display. When they came to the children's clothing stores, Reb Shlomo was totally entranced.

"Let's go in here a minute," he said to Reb David as he stepped into one of the shops. Inside were rows of attractively styled boys' suits in dark blues, grays, and blacks. Reb Shlomo fingered one with shiny, gold buttons and held it up for Reb David to see.

"How I'd love to buy such a suit for my

Avraimeleh," he sighed, "but I'm afraid it wouldn't
fit him. What a shame I can't tell what size he
needs. If it turns out to be too small, it would just
be a waste of good money. I guess there's no point
in taking a chance."

Reb Shlomo longingly turned the suit this way
and that, wistfully picturing his only son in it.
Finally, he hung it back on the rack with a sigh
of resignation.

While Reb Shlomo had been lost in thoughts
of his Avraimeleh, Reb David had not stood by
idly. Three carefully selected boys' suits, in different sizes, were neatly folded on the counter, and
Reb David was busy bargaining with the shop
owner for a good price.

Suddenly realizing what his friend was up to, Reb
Shlomo asked in surprise: "But how do you know
what size to buy? What will you do if they don't fit?"

"I understand your question," answered the
younger man, taking care not to offend Reb
Shlomo. "But, *baruch Hashem*, I have five boys at
home, so what doesn't fit my Yankeleh might fit
my Leibeleh or my Shimon. And if one suit doesn't
fit any of them, well, I'm still young, and perhaps
the *Ribbono Shel Olam* will give me more children,
so I'll put it away for one of them to grow into.

"Your situation is different. It doesn't make
sense for you to take a chance and buy for your

Avraimeleh, because he's an only child. But for me, it would be a waste *not* to purchase such fine outfits. They're bound to fit someone in the family sooner or later."

All the challenges that Avraham Avinu faced were for the benefit of the generations that would later descend from the holy *Avos.* For instance, Hashem sent *malachim* to Avraham Avinu just after his *bris milah.* Not only was Avraham still recuperating, but Hashem made it a very hot day; even so, Avraham Avinu himself waited on the visitors, treating them like royal guests.

Later, when Avraham Avinu's descendants were on their way to Eretz Yisrael from Mitzrayim, the entire nation benefitted from this good deed: because Avraham Avinu himself had served the *malachim* hundreds of years beforehand, Hashem Himself provided the Jewish people with manna in the desert for forty years.

Hashem knew that Avraham Avinu excelled in the *middah* of *chesed,* and that as soon as he heard entire cities were in danger of being destroyed, he would plead for them. Hashem also knew that Avraham Avinu's prayers would not save Sedom and Amorah. Even so, He wanted Avraham Avinu to pray.

Why?

Because Avraham Avinu was to become the father of a "great and mighty nation"; he would have many, many descendants to "try on" the merits he had acquired. If those *zechuyos* didn't fit one of his children or grandchildren, they would surely fit another, like the three suits that Reb David bought in the Maggid's story.

The father of a large family, of a great nation, provides for all his children and grandchildren. Thus, Avraham Avinu "stored up" *zechuyos* for the generations to follow. Even though Sedom and Amorah were not saved, Avraham's prayers were not, *chas vechalilah*, for nought. Hashem wanted those prayers not for the benefit of Sedom and Amorah, right there and then, but for the future benefit of *klal Yisrael*, the "great and mighty nation" that would descend from Avraham Avinu. That's why He revealed to Avraham Avinu what was about to happen to Sedom and Amorah, giving him an opportunity to daven for them.

The vast merit of all the *Avos'* prayers, mitzvos, and great deeds remains our priceless inheritance to this very day. And to this day, Jews throughout the world turn to Hashem each day and ask: "For the sake of our forefathers, who trusted in You, and You taught them the laws of life, so, too, be gracious with us and teach us...."

Chayei Sarah

When Gain is Loss

וַיִּשְׁמַע אַבְרָהָם אֶל עֶפְרוֹן וַיִּשְׁקֹל אַבְרָהָם לְעֶפְרֹן אֶת
הַכֶּסֶף....

*Avraham listened to Efron, and Avraham
weighed out the money for Efron....*
(Bereishis 23:16)

WHEN AVRAHAM AVINU returned from
the *akeidah* and found that Sarah Im-
einu had died, he had to acquire a
gravesite. So he asked Efron to sell him his field,
which included the cave of Machpeilah.

But Efron would not *sell* the field to Avraham
Avinu. Rather, he wanted to *give* it to him as a
present: "No, my lord, hear me: I give you the field;
and the cave that is in it, I give to you. Bury your
dead" (Bereishis 23:11).

However, Avraham Avinu refused the gift. He

again told Efron that he wanted to *buy* the field: "But if you would only hear me: I will give the price of the field; take it from me and I will bury my dead there" (23:13).

Efron realized this was a chance to make a large profit. Therefore, even though in the beginning he had offered to give the field away as a present, now he asked an extremely high price for it: four hundred shekels.

Despite the high price, "Avraham weighed out the money for Efron" (23:16).

Throughout the story, Efron's name is spelled with a *vav*, but in the phrase "the money for Efron," there is no *vav*. Why?

Furthermore, a midrash on this verse quotes a *pasuk* from Mishlei: "A man of evil eye rushes after wealth and does not know that a loss will come his way" (28:22). "A man of evil eye" — this is Efron, the *midrash* tells us. It is not difficult to understand why the greedy Efron, who used his eyes to look for a way to make money, is called a "man of evil eye." But what does the second half of the verse — "a loss will come his way" — mean? Didn't Efron *gain* four hundred shekels?

The Dubno Maggid explains with a *mashal*:

One evening, as the famous Lord Bensham and his men were making their way south to join the king at his winter court in Heissenburgh, they spotted a pleasant-looking inn off to the side of the road. The neatly painted sign seemed to beckon to them: "Coatsworth Arms, Geoffrey Whitehall, Proprietor." Lord Bensham suddenly recalled how long they had been on the road and how empty their insides were.

"Stanford, tell the men to halt. We'll turn in here for the night. It looks like as good a place as any."

"Yes, m'lord," Stanford nodded. He signaled the others to follow him up the path leading to Coatsworth Arms. Then he galloped ahead towards the inn to make the arrangements.

"Hello, my good man," he greeted the inn-keeper. "Prepare your best rooms. You've the honor of hosting Lord Bensham and his men. His Lordship is tired and hungry and won't be kept waiting. Treat him well and you won't regret it."

Delighted to host such an aristocratic guest, and eager to earn a fat profit, Geoffrey Whitehall rushed to the kitchen to urge the staff into rapid action:

"Harris, go out and stable their horses, and you, Marsy, get ready to serve up a royal banquet. Tell Thomas to fetch the best wines from the cellar. Take out the finest dishes and cutlery, and use that new linen cloth the weaver just delivered."

Geoffrey quickly washed his face, donned his

best coat, and greeted Lord Bensham with a low bow and a warm welcome.

"What an extraordinary honor for us, Your Lordship. Welcome to Coatsworth Arms. We'll offer you the finest cuisine, elegant suites, and — "

Lord Bensham interrupted Geoffrey's welcome speech by returning his greeting politely but briefly, and asking where he might find the dining hall. Right now he was interested in a good meal and a rest, not curtsies and compliments.

Geoffrey assured the guests that he would serve them a meal they would not soon forget, and led the way to the dining room.

The meal was much enjoyed by all, and afterward Lord Bensham thanked Geoffrey and praised his staff's cooking.

"Ah," thought Geoffrey to himself, "it was worth all the effort. His Lordship enjoyed himself, and he is known to be both wealthy and generous. If all goes well, this evening's work will bring us a handsome profit."

The next morning Geoffrey was up before dawn to oversee the preparations for breakfast. Again he played the gracious host and won Lord Bensham's praise for the inn's hospitality.

At last it was time for the guests to leave. Lord Bensham sent Stanford to ask Geoffrey for a reckoning of how much was due.

This was the moment Geoffrey had been waiting for. Without hesitation, he listed each item and its price, neatly recording the figures for His Lordship to see. The total bill came to a substantial amount.

Stanford's eyebrows rose in surprise but he said nothing. It was not his place to comment; he would leave that to his master.

Lord Bensham's expression momentarily mirrored Stanford's when he heard the sum Geoffrey had requested. But he was certainly too well-bred — and too wealthy — to make an issue of it.

"Give him what he wants," he ordered, "and let's be off."

The distinguished guests departed, leaving Geoffrey to count his fortune again and again with great delight.

Once on the road, Lord Bensham soon forgot both Geoffrey and his inn, turning his thoughts to several matters he hoped to discuss with the king once they arrived at his winter headquarters. But his deliberations were cut short by a rumble of thunder. All eyes turned to the horizon, where dark, gray storm clouds left no doubts: they had to find shelter at once.

"I think I see a large building on ahead. Shall we try for it, m'lord?" Stanford asked.

"Right!" answered His Lordship. "Tell the others."

The rain caught them shortly before they

reached their destination, which turned out to be a small inn.

The owner of the Golden Lamb, Ernest Reit, welcomed them and assured His Lordship that he would do everything he could to make their stay a pleasant one. Then, without another word, he went to arrange for a steaming hot meal to warm the travelers' chilled bones. He understood that now was not the time for flowery speeches; pot roast and potatoes would say more to His Lordship than any words of praise and appreciation.

A short while later, Ernest reappeared and graciously guided the hungry men into the dining hall, where the cook and her helpers were just adding the finishing touches to the dinner table. A platter of fresh rolls filled the room with a delicious aroma, and the tantalizing smell of a juicy roast wafted in from the kitchen.

The travelers wasted no time; they fell on the food with gusto. Ernest deftly supervised the serving of the meal from beginning to end, always ready to provide a bit more gravy here or refill an empty glass there.

Once they had finished their meal, Ernest led them to a cozy parlor, where a roaring fire had warmed the room for them while they were eating. A generous supply of cake and ale awaited them on the sideboard. The friendly crackle of the fire warmed their spirits and helped them forget the dreary weather.

Ernest left the men around the fireplace and went upstairs to supervise the preparation of the finest suites. He made sure each member of the staff knew his job and did it well:

"You, Margaret, open the northern suite and ready it. Use the finest linens we have and be sure the rooms are spotless. You, Thomas, fetch several buckets of fresh springwater."

Then Ernest returned to His Lordship downstairs to ask whether there was anything else he might do for him. Lord Bensham thanked him warmly and asked whether they might retire soon so as to get an early start the next morning.

"Just another few moments, Your Lordship, and I trust all will be ready."

Ernest raced back upstairs to inspect the bedrooms personally.

"How often do we have the honor of entertaining nobility?" he reminded himself. "I must be sure there is nothing missing and nothing amiss."

Not long afterward, Lord Bensham's party were all slumbering peacefully.

The next morning dawned bright and fair, and after a pleasant breakfast, they were ready to leave. As usual, Lord Bensham sent Stanford to settle the account.

"Payment?" echoed Ernest. "No payment is necessary, unless it is I who am required to pay His Lordship for the privilege of serving him. From the beginning, I had no intention of accepting payment for my humble hospitality."

Somewhat surprised, Stanford relayed the response to Lord Bensham, who asked that Ernest come speak to him in person.

"We've been very cozy and comfortable here at the Golden Lamb, Ernest, and I'd like to pay you your due for your good services."

"How can I possibly accept payment, Your Lordship, when it is I who have been the recipient? I cannot begin to tell you what a pleasure it has been for me to serve you, and to be of some small assistance to a noble of Your Lordship's stature."

"Very well," said Lord Bensham, obviously touched by Ernest's words. "Then let me offer you a token of our friendship. You won't deny me that small pleasure, will you?"

"No, my lord, of course not; it is only my lord's pleasure that I seek," replied Ernest.

"Then it is agreed," answered Lord Bensham with a smile. "Stanford, fetch the silver snuffbox from my room." Turning to Ernest he explained: "It will be yours to remember me by."

At a loss for words, Ernest could only sputter, "Thank you. I shall treasure it always as a precious reminder of the deep pleasure Your Lordship's presence has afforded us."

Stanford returned with a jewel-studded snuff-box that took Ernest's breath away. Inlaid with diamonds and rubies, it was worth far, far more than any innkeeper's paltry bill for one night's hospitality. But he dared not protest; he had agreed to accept it, and to refuse would be an insult.

Again he thanked His Lordship and wished him good health and a safe journey.

After the guests had gone, one of Ernest's sons asked: "Father, is it true that you didn't want Lord Bensham to pay you, even though he has more money than your other guests?"

"Yes, it's true. I wanted to serve him out of respect for his greatness, not in order to earn money.

"But in the end, I only gained, because the present he left me is worth far, far more than what he would have paid for staying here one night. I'll never forget him."

Ernest wasn't the only one who didn't forget. Two months later, when Lord Bensham was on his way back from the king's palace, he had forgotten Geoffrey Whitehall altogether, but he remembered Ernest Reit fondly. So fondly, in fact, that he stopped again at the Golden Lamb. This time he didn't even try to pay Ernest; instead he presented him — and his children — with more presents.

And the following year it happened again: Each time he was near the Golden Lamb, he made a point of visiting, at least for a meal. And each time, he would leave an expensive gift in appreciation for Ernest's devoted service and concern, a gift that far outweighed any expenses the innkeeper incurred from his visits.

Geoffrey, who was so anxious to become rich, was long forgotten; but Ernest, who wanted only the pleasure of serving a noble aristocrat, had his wish fulfilled again and again, and became rich at the same time.

Efron was like Geoffrey in the *mashal*. Both men wanted to profit by charging more than a fair price. Both thought they were gaining, but they were actually losing out.

In the *mashal*, we clearly see what Geoffrey lost to Ernest: fine, expensive presents from Lord Bensham, year after year — and, even more important, the friendship and admiration of a great person.

But what did Efron lose by overcharging for his field?

The Maggid explains: Sometimes Hashem gives a person an opportunity to play an important role in history, one that will cause his name to be remembered for good and bring him untold merit. Betzalel was given the chance to play such a role when Hashem called him by name and "...filled him with the spirit of Hashem, with wisdom, with understanding, with knowledge, and with all kinds of craftsmanship" (Shemos 31:2).

Betzalel used his special opportunity to please Hashem as much as he could. He fashioned the *mishkan* as Hashem wanted it to be. The Maggid writes that this was a wonderful *zechus* for him because the *mishkan* pleased Hashem very much, and each time He "remembered" it, He would remember Betzalel favorably as well.

Efron was also given a chance to be remembered for good. His field could have been called "*sedei Efron*," Efron's field, if he had realized that here was a chance for him to do something great by helping a great person, Avraham Avinu, whom his people called "a prince of God in our midst" (Bereishis 23:6). Efron knew that Avraham Avinu was a great and noble person, and that Heaven was giving him a chance to help a tzaddik. His name would always have been remembered for good as someone who had helped a righteous person in his time of need.

But "a man of evil eye rushes after wealth":

Instead of running after *zechuyos*, Efron ran after money. Like Geoffrey, he lost his chance. The field lost the name *sedei Efron*, as the *Chumash* tells us: "And the field of Efron...became the property of Avraham..." (23:17-18).

Efron was too busy thinking of riches to seize this golden opportunity to gain eternal merit. Therefore, as the *pasuk* in Mishlei warns us, a loss came his way. The Torah hints at this loss by writing Efron's name with the "loss" of a *vav* precisely when Avraham Avinu paid him the four hundred silver shekels for his field.

The Torah teaches us not to be like Efron, who rushed to gain silver coins, but rather to use every opportunity Hashem sends us to serve Him.

Toldos

The Secret of Eisav/Edom's Power

...וְאֶת אָחִיךָ תַּעֲבֹד וְהָיָה כַּאֲשֶׁר תָּרִיד וּפָרַקְתָּ עֻלּוֹ מֵעַל צַוָּארֶךָ.

...and you (Eisav) shall serve your brother (Yaakov), but it shall come to pass that when you grieve, you shall cast his yoke from off your neck.

(Bereishis 27:40)

W E ALL KNOW that *klal Yisrael* is very dear to Hashem and that He watches over us continuously. We are even compared to a father's firstborn child, as Hashem says, "*Bni bechori Yisrael*— Israel is My firstborn" (Shemos 4:22).

Yet various nations have mistreated the Jewish people and caused vast suffering.

The Romans, who were descended from Eisav,

tortured and murdered thousands of *talmidei chachamim*, including Rabbi Akiva and nine of his colleagues. They slew approximately one million Jews, and exiled and enslaved one hundred thousand more. They defiled Hashem's holy Temple and burned it to the ground. Like their forefather Eisav, they were evil and cruel through and through.

Yet, throughout history, countries like Rome have prospered. Their armies are feared far and wide, their statesmen, generals, artists, and scientists become world-famous — and all this even though they do not care a bit about keeping the mitzvos Hashem gave them.

Why does Hashem allow wicked nations to enjoy such strength and power? Why should we have to see Eisav's children strutting proudly around as though they owned the world and were the most righteous people on the face of the earth?

We find the answer in *parashas Toldos*: "...and you shall serve your brother..." (Bereishis 27:40). Yitzchak Avinu tells Eisav that his descendants — Edom — will serve their brothers, the sons of Yaakov. But "...it shall come to pass that when you grieve [when Israel violates the Torah, Eisav will have reason to grieve over the blessings the Jews have received — Rashi], you shall cast his yoke from off your neck."

Chazal tell us that when we truly keep Torah and mitzvos, it is we who will rule over the other nations; Edom won't be able to harm us. But if we become lax in our observance, Eisav — and the nations descended from him — will become world powers and gain control over us. Since Eisav's descendants hate us just as Eisav himself hated Yaakov Avinu, they use their power to hurt us as much as they possibly can.

To explain why Hashem gives Eisav this temporary power and glory, the Dubno Maggid uses one of his famous *mashalim*:

A kind-hearted and wise king once had a son whom he loved more than anything else in the world. The king assigned the best servants and nursemaids to look after him. Whenever he was hungry, he received wholesome, tasty meals; whenever he wanted to play, the servants gave him whatever games he fancied. The best tailors made him elegant, warm clothes, and the most brilliant tutors made his studies enjoyable. In short, he was surrounded by a loving family and staff who were only too happy to fulfill his every wish.

Despite the wonderful care the prince received, he became so ill that even the most skilled physicians despaired of finding a cure. Famous doctors, summoned to the palace from afar, shook their heads and sadly told the king that his son would not live much longer.

Only one white-haired professor thought there might be some hope.

"I shall try to cure your son," he told the king, "but only if you promise me two things. First, you must not come near the prince while I am caring for him, because in your presence I will not have the strength to make him take the bitter medicines he needs to save his life.

"Second, I want you to send away all the prince's personal staff. Until now, he has been waited upon by good-hearted people who love him and generously do whatever they can to make him happy. Now you must find someone selfish and cruel to look after him—the meaner, the better. Only someone with a heart of stone can do the job.

"This person will have to force the prince to take his medicines — even though they are terribly bitter — and to undergo painful treatments. He will also have to stop the prince from eating the foods he likes, which keep the medicines from working. Anyone who loves the prince will take pity on him and will not do the job well enough to save his life. You must search throughout your kingdom for men of evil disposition, choosing the fiercest, strictest ones to look after the prince until he recovers."

With no other hope of saving his beloved son's life, the king agreed. At once he sent messengers to every corner of his kingdom to find hard-hearted bullies and bring them back to the palace.

The messengers returned with just the right type of people. Not only were they fierce-looking, but they were proud of it. They could not stop bragging about how the king had summoned them to the palace to cure the prince.

At last one of the king's ministers could no longer stand it, and hushed their boasting.

"Arrogant fools! Do you think it is because you are such fine fellows that the king has brought you here? Don't be such dunces! Right now, the king has no choice but to give you the job because the prince is so sick and you are so beastly cruel. You will not heed the boy's pleas for mercy, and will force him to take his medicines just as the doctor prescribed. It is because you are so mean and heartless that you are here, not because you are better than others. As soon as the prince is well again, the king will throw you out on your ears, ruffians that you are!"

Similarly, we find the prophet Ovadiah addressing Edom, the nation of Eisav:

"Behold, I have appointed you the least of the

nations; you are greatly despised. [But] the arrogance of your heart has raised you on high like one who dwells in the clefts of the rock and says in his heart, 'Who will cast me down to earth?' " (Ovadiah 1:2-3).

Sometimes *klal Yisrael* becomes "ill" — failing to keep Torah and mitzvos as Hashem wants — and our Father, the King, calls in the cruel sons of Eisav to administer the treatments required to heal us. This is not a mark of distinction for Eisav, but rather a way to make use of his cruelty and evil ways for our benefit. Wicked nations mistakenly think that Hashem has deemed them superior to His "firstborn," Israel. They fail to realize that their new status is temporary, that even if they seem to conquer the very heavens, in the end they will fall, as the *navi* continues: "Even if you rise high like the eagle, if you place your nest amongst the stars, from there I shall bring you down, says Hashem" (Ovadiah 1:4).

Thus, when we see Eisav/Edom become a great power and conquer the world, we should remember that Hashem is behind it all, arranging things for our benefit. If we but return to Hashem with all our hearts, the cruel taskmaster of Edom will be banished from the palace forever. Then we will be free to serve Hashem with happy hearts, amid peace and plenty, and Hashem will again shower His blessings on us without end.

VaYeitzei

The Time of Redemption

וַיַּחֲלֹם וְהִנֵּה סֻלָּם מֻצָּב אַרְצָה וְרֹאשׁוֹ מַגִּיעַ הַשָּׁמָיְמָה וְהִנֵּה
מַלְאֲכֵי אֱלֹקִים עֹלִים וְיֹרְדִים בּוֹ.

*And [Yaakov] dreamed: and behold, a ladder
was set up on earth, and the top of it reached
to heaven; and behold, angels of God were
ascending and descending on it.*

(Bereishis 28:12)

Y AAKOV AVINU DREAMT that the angels of
various nations were going up and down a
ladder. The angel of Bavel mounted 70
rungs because our exile there would last 70 years.
The angel of Madai climbed 52 rungs before he
came back down, and the angel of Greece rose 180
rungs. Thus Yaakov Avinu knew how long his
descendants would be exiled in each country, and
he was sure that eventually each exile would come

to an end. Sooner or later, his children would return to their homeland and rejoice.

The last angel to climb the ladder was that of Eisav's nation, Edom. Yaakov Avinu watched as the angel climbed 50, 100, 150, 200 rungs — and carried on. There was no end. Would his sons never be redeemed from the cruel hands of his brother Eisav?

Hashem reassured him that even if Eisav's descendants "rose on high like the eagle, or placed [their] nest among the stars, [He] would eventually bring them down from there..." (Ovadiah 1:4). But Hashem didn't reveal to Yaakov how long *galus Edom* — our present exile — would last.

The Dubno Maggid explains why with a *mashal*:

A wealthy man once died very young, leaving everything he owned to his only son. Since the boy was too young to manage the property on his own, the court appointed a guardian to do so.

The guardian decided first of all to rent out the huge mansion in which the family lived. As soon as the news spread that the beautiful mansion was for rent, the four richest families in town all begged the guardian to lease it to them. A bitter fight broke out among the four families. Each insisted that it was first in line to rent the house.

"Why fight?" exclaimed the guardian. "It will be years and years until the boy is old enough to live here himself. Meanwhile, there's time enough for all four of you to live here, if only you will agree to take turns."

So they sat down to make a schedule. The first three families to rent the mansion were each given contracts specifying exactly how long they would be entitled to the beautiful home. In the fourth family's contract, however, no specific date was set for vacating the property. The guardian could not say so many years in advance when the owner — now just a young boy — would be mature enough to take over his estate. So the fourth contract just said that the family would move out whenever the owner himself was ready to move in.

So it is with *klal Yisrael*. We have been sent into exile until we are "mature" enough and righteous enough to deserve *geulah*. How many years that will take depends on the quality of our mitzvos and Torah learning. Hashem did not show Yaakov Avinu the time of the final redemption because He wanted us to strive daily to achieve it — may it come speedily in our days!

VaYishlach

Blessings in Disguise

...עִם לָבָן גַּרְתִּי וָאֵחַר עַד עָתָּה. וַיְהִי לִי שׁוֹר וַחֲמוֹר צֹאן
וְעֶבֶד וְשִׁפְחָה וָאֶשְׁלְחָה לְהַגִּיד לַאדֹנִי לִמְצֹא חֵן בְּעֵינֶיךָ.

*I [Yaakov] have lived with Lavan and tarried
till now. And I have oxen and donkeys and
flocks and menservants and maidservants,
and I am sending [word] to my master [Eisav]
to find favor in your eyes.*

(Bereishis 32:5-6)

THIRTY-FOUR YEARS had passed since
Yaakov Avinu fled from his twin brother,
Eisav, who was determined to kill him for
taking the *berachos* from their father, Yitzchak
Avinu.

Yaakov Avinu knew what awaited him now
that he was coming back to Eretz Yisrael with his

wives and children. He knew that Eisav still wanted revenge. We would think, then, that Yaakov would have tried to hide at least some of his vast wealth from jealous Eisav. But instead, Yaakov Avinu went out of his way to tell his brother all about his riches. Why?

Another strange point: Yaakov Avinu told Eisav that until now he had stayed with Lavan. What difference could that have made to Eisav?

And why did Yaakov Avinu preface his description of his riches with the word *vayehi* ("and there is" [to me]), which implies something that has just come into being, as in "*vayehi ohr*" — "and there was light" (Bereishis 1:3)?

The Dubno Maggid answers all these questions with a *mashal*:

A businessman named Reuven had fallen on hard times. No one was buying from him, and week after week he lost more and more money. He decided that he had no choice but to try something drastic.

A friend had once told him about a distant island where traders came from the four corners of the earth with exotic spices, fabrics, and jewels. The merchants sold their goods at low prices because they were in such a hurry that they didn't bother bargaining. Anyone who took the trouble to travel to this island could make a fortune, his friend told him.

So off Reuven went. But things didn't work out the way Reuven's friend had predicted. Whatever he tried to sell, twenty other fellows began to sell more cheaply. He tried textiles, jewels, and spices, but something always went wrong. Months became years and still Reuven's purse was nearly empty. Years passed, but he became no wealthier.

At last Reuven decided he had had enough. So he scrounged together what little he had, sold what he could, and bought a ticket on the next ship home.

Two days before Reuven was to leave, an important-looking stranger ran up to him and said: "They tell me you are honest. Do you want to make some money? Here, take this casket of gems and sell it for me in town. I don't have time to do it myself. I have to stay here with the ship. Come back with the money by tomorrow morning, and half of it will be yours." Without another word, the stranger thrust the casket into Reuven's hands and disappeared.

Reuven opened the casket and took a good look at its contents. The exquisite diamonds, rubies, and sapphires took his breath away, and his head started to spin at the thought of the money they would bring.

After all these years, Reuven knew all the gem dealers on the island. He knew what to offer to whom, and he bargained well. The jewels brought in such a huge sum that Reuven had to pinch himself to be sure it wasn't a dream.

Shortly after dawn the next morning, Reuven paid the stranger his half of the money. A day later, Reuven headed for home laden with fabulous presents for his family and friends. There was a smile on his face and a fat purse in his pocket.

When he reached his hometown, he received a royal welcome.

"Just look at those clothes!" everyone cried.

"Have you seen the rings and necklaces and fine silks Reuven brought his wife and daughters? Where did he say that island is? I'm leaving tomorrow to make my fortune!"

"Not so fast, my friends," Reuven told them. "Before you buy your tickets, let me tell you what happened to me while I was away.

"For years I tried to make my fortune. I bought, I sold, I traded and traveled, I asked and watched others, and I learned all the tricks of the trade — but I made hardly a penny. When I decided at last to come home, I had to sell nearly everything I owned just to buy my ticket.

"Then, just two days before I left, an unbelievable deal fell into my lap. It was nothing less than a miracle. All those years I sweated and toiled for nothing, and then in a few hours I became the fabulously rich man you see before you. It was a fantastic stroke of good luck, a gift from Heaven.

"So don't waste your time and money running away to some island to seek your fortune; Heaven can send you good luck right here at home, too."

For twenty years, Yaakov Avinu worked day and night for Lavan. But he himself remained poor. Despite the *berachah* he had received instead of Eisav, despite the *bechorah* he had bought from his brother, Yaakov had nothing to show for twenty years of hard labor. As Yaakov Avinu said to Lavan: "Were it not for the God of my father...you would have sent me away now empty-handed..." (Bereishis 31:42). It was only because Hashem had blessed Yaakov with vast wealth that he now appeared before Eisav as a rich man.

This is what Yaakov Avinu wanted Eisav to understand: His wealth was a present direct from Hashem, not the result of the *berachos* their father had given him. Therefore, there was no reason for Eisav to be jealous, and nothing to rekindle the hatred that burned in his heart.

As Yaakov told Eisav, "I have oxen and don-

keys and flocks and menservants and maidservants" — through a sudden miracle performed by
Hashem. "And I am sending [word] to tell my
master to find favor in your eyes" — I want you to
know that I became wealthy through a miracle so
you won't be angry with me for taking your
berachah."

VaYeishev

The Baker's Dream

בְּעוֹד שְׁלֹשֶׁת יָמִים יִשָּׂא פַרְעֹה אֶת רֹאשְׁךָ מֵעָלֶיךָ וְתָלָה אוֹתְךָ
עַל עֵץ וְאָכַל הָעוֹף אֶת בְּשָׂרְךָ מֵעָלֶיךָ.

*In another three days Pharaoh will lift up your
head from off you and hang you on a tree, and
the birds will eat your flesh from off you.*
(Bereishis 40:19)

FTER YOSEF'S OPTIMISTIC interpretation of the chief butler's dream ("in another three days Pharaoh will raise up
your head and restore you to your position..."
[Bereishis 40:13]), the chief baker was eager to
submit his own dream to Yosef's scrutiny. But the
interpretation he received was very different: In
three days he was to be hanged!

How did Yosef know that this was to be the
chief baker's fate?

The Dubno Maggid explains with a *mashal*:

An outstanding artist once painted a beautiful picture of a man holding a bowl of fruit. The apples, pears, grapes, and cherries looked so real that people came from near and far to see them.

When the town held an outdoor exhibition to display its greatest works of art, the painting became a special center of attraction: The fruit looked real not only to people, but even to the birds flying overhead. Visitors would stand around, still as statues, watching all kinds of birds land on the painting and start pecking away at the crimson cherries, yellow-green pears, and shiny, juicy-looking, red apples. Only after a few good pecks at the canvas would the birds give up hope of a luscious meal and fly away. Then all the spectators would exclaim: "Perfect! Amazing! I've never seen anything like it!"

Even the mayor was delighted, for his town was becoming famous. So perfect was this work of art that he offered a grand prize to anyone who could find the slightest flaw in it.

Now even more people came to see the celebrated picture. Who didn't want to win a grand prize? But they were all stumped. What could possibly be wrong with a painting that fooled even the sharp-eyed birds?

No one came forward with a single complaint...until one clever fellow claimed he had truly found fault with the picture.

"Look," he said, "if I were to stand here in the town square with a bowl of fruit in my hands, not one bird would come peck at it, no matter how tempting my cherries and grapes looked. But the birds do try to eat the fruit in the picture. Why? Because the portrait of the man holding the bowl doesn't look real to them, so they're not afraid to land right on his hand and start pecking away."

Everyone had to agree. There was no question that the fruit was a masterpiece, but the picture of the man was just that — only a picture. The man won his prize.

The chief baker's dream was similar to this picture. As he told Yosef: "...in my dream, behold, there were three woven baskets over my head. And in the top basket there were all kinds of baked goods for Pharaoh, and the birds were eating them from the basket over my head" (Bereishis 40:16-17).

Because the man they saw — the chief baker — didn't look lifelike to them, the birds were not afraid to eat right out of the basket over his head. In his dream, the baker was just a *picture* of himself, not a real, living person. In other words, in three days he would no longer *be* a real, living person.

And so it was, as the *pasuk* tells us:

"... and the chief baker, he [Pharaoh] hanged, as Yosef had foretold to them" (40:22).

MiKeitz

The Doctor No One Liked

וְעַתָּה יֵרֶא פַרְעֹה אִישׁ נָבוֹן וְחָכָם וִישִׁיתֵהוּ עַל אֶרֶץ מִצְרָיִם.
יַעֲשֶׂה פַרְעֹה וְיַפְקֵד פְּקִדִים עַל הָאָרֶץ וְחִמֵּשׁ אֶת אֶרֶץ מִצְרַיִם
בְּשֶׁבַע שְׁנֵי הַשָּׂבָע.

And now, let Pharaoh look for an understanding, wise person and put him in charge of Egypt. Let Pharaoh act and appoint officers over the land and set aside a fifth [of the produce] of the land of Egypt during the seven years of plenty.

(Bereishis 41:33-34)

WITH THE GUIDANCE of Hashem, Yosef HaTzaddik has just explained to Pharaoh the meaning of his strange dream: Seven years of plenty will be followed by seven years of famine. But Yosef does not stop there. He proceeds to tell Pharaoh how to solve the problems the famine will bring.

It seems strange that Yosef, who only hours before had been a lowly prisoner, is now giving the mighty Pharaoh suggestions on how to run the country. Surely there was no shortage of advisors and counselors in Pharaoh's court. In fact, having been summoned to try to interpret the mysterious dream, they were all standing there waiting to hear what the Jewish prisoner would say. Wasn't Yosef afraid of angering them by advising Pharaoh while they were all waiting to do the same?

The Dubno Maggid explains what Yosef had in mind with a *mashal*:

Once there was a king whose son became deathly ill. The court physician could not find any way to heal him, nor could the other experts who were called in. The king became so desperate that he sent royal messengers to proclaim throughout the land that anyone who might be able to help should come to the palace at once. It didn't matter to the king whether one was a doctor, a magician, or a sorcerer. The main thing was that the prince be cured.

Usually no one was allowed into the private chambers of the palace, but the king instructed the guards to let any expert into the prince's room to examine him, if only it might help him get better.

One doctor in the capital was very smart, but he was not at all popular. He did things differently than the other doctors, so they thought him odd. People admitted that he knew a great deal, but they disliked his strange ways and stayed away from him.

When the prince first became ill, this doctor had not gone to the palace to help. He was quite sure that he could cure the boy with a common herb that grew along every river bank. But why should he go argue with the medical authorities who had come from near and far if they would refuse to listen to him?

Now, however, the situation had changed. The king had opened the doors of the palace to every expert in the kingdom. Now there was a way to examine the prince without everyone arguing with him.

So the doctor went to examine the prince in person, and saw that he had indeed been right about the cure. Eager to save the prince, he went to tell the king.

But when he got to the throne room, he found the king surrounded by doctors and professors from many countries. Some of them had even brought whole cases of rare medicines with them.

But when he got to the throne room, he found the king surrounded by doctors and professors from many countries.

The king might have been willing to listen to him, but the other doctors would surely make fun of his diagnosis and the common, everyday medicine he wanted to prescribe. He had to think of some way to make the others agree with him and recommend his treatment to the king.

What did he do?

First he asked permission to speak to the king and all the physicians in the room. Then he told them what he thought the problem was. Finally, he explained which medicine would cure the prince's illness. But he did not stop there. He told the king that the herb had to be prepared by a great expert who could grind it up just the right way. The king must search for a gifted pharmacist who was skilled at preparing rare, exotic medications. Only then could he be sure that the prince would be cured.

The doctor did not fail to mention that such an expert would deserve a generous reward for his work.

As the physicians stood listening, each thought to himself, "Surely the king will ask me to do the job since I have such a fine reputation. Therefore, I must urge the king to accept this fellow's advice."

And so it was that everyone suddenly agreed with the strange doctor, even though they did not like him and his odd ways. They all encouraged the king to give the suggested cure a try, thinking of the hefty reward they would earn for grinding the herb.

But much to their disappointment, to prepare the medicine the king chose none other than the strange doctor himself!

"You must be the greatest expert of all!" the king declared. "Of all the doctors I have consulted, only you proposed this cure. No one can compare to you. So you yourself will be the one to prepare the herb."

Yosef HaTzaddik had a similar difficulty. He was a lowly prisoner. In addition, he was a foreigner, different from the Egyptians. And not only was he different, but he was an *Ivri,* a Hebrew, whom the Egyptians detested. How could he convince Pharaoh's advisors to agree with his interpretation of the dream? By suggesting that the king appoint a supervisor over the entire country. Each of the ministers was sure that he would be the one chosen.

But of course, Hashem wanted it otherwise. Yosef was the one Hashem wanted to raise to power. Therefore He made Pharaoh decide: "...there is no one as wise and understanding as you" (41:39).

VaYigash

The Duke's Sapphire

וְעַתָּה אַל תֵּעָצְבוּ וְאַל יִחַר בְּעֵינֵיכֶם כִּי מְכַרְתֶּם אֹתִי הֵנָּה
כִּי לְמִחְיָה שְׁלָחַנִי אֱלֹקִים לִפְנֵיכֶם.

*And now, don't be sad, and don't be angry
with yourselves that you sold me here, for
Hashem sent me before you to preserve life.*
(Bereishis 45:5)

AFTER YEARS OF tragic separation, Yosef
and his brothers have found each other
again.

Yosef is overjoyed and grateful to Hashem. But
the brothers are frightened: Will Yosef be angry
with them for having sold him to the Yishmaelites
when he was only seventeen? Will he resent all
the pain they caused Yaakov, their father?
Twenty-two years ago, they scoffed at his dreams,
but now those dreams have come true: they them-

selves have bowed down to the mighty ruler of Egypt, who turns out to be none other than their long-lost brother, Yosef! They are speechless with shame, and fear Yosef's reaction.

But Yosef's words (see above) reveal no anger. In fact, he continues: "For it is two years now that there is a famine in the land, and there will be another five years in which there will be no plowing and harvest.... So now it was not you who sent me here, but Hashem, and He has placed me as a father to Pharaoh and as a master over all his house, and a ruler over all the land of Egypt" (Bereishis 45:6, 8).

Why does Yosef give such a lengthy explanation to his brothers? What does he want them to understand?

The Dubno Maggid answers with a *mashal*:

There was once a wealthy duke who owned a fabulous sapphire, the largest and most exquisite in the whole duchy. The duke took great pride in his gem; everyone knew that no other stone in the realm could compare with it. The sapphire made the duke feel important and distinguished. Nobles considered it a privilege to gape at its indescribable beauty.

Of course, the duke guarded his treasure zealously, but even so, something went wrong:

One day two visitors asked to see the gem. Carefully the duke opened his silver jewel box and lifted out the famous stone. As he unwrapped it, he suddenly gasped: "Oh no! It can't be! My sapphire! It's split!"

The visitors bent over and peered at the gem in the duke's hand. Sure enough, a deep, ugly crack ran straight across the face of the magnificent jewel.

"How did it happen? It's not possible! How could it get damaged just sitting in a padded case?" the duke wailed.

No one had an answer for the duke, and in any case no explanation could repair the damage. The question was what to do with the stone now.

The duke decided to consult the greatest experts in the kingdom. Gem cutters, polishers, and jewelers from near and far were summoned to the castle. What an honor to be the one to find a way to repair the duke's famous gem, they thought. And what a handsome reward the duke would surely bestow upon the expert who succeeded in restoring the precious sapphire to its splendor!

But no one could find a way. One after another, they examined the famous stone and sadly shook their heads in defeat.

"It just can't be done," one concluded.

"Even if I polish it, there will always be a mark

where the split was," said another.

"The best I can do is make it look like just a scratch," ventured a third craftsman.

The duke was despondent. Was there no hope, no trick of the trade that could save his incomparable gem?

At last one expert had an idea that showed some promise. After examining the sapphire at length, he turned to the duke with a deep bow.

"If my lord desires, I shall engrave a magnificent design on the face of the stone. When the design is complete, the stone will be even more exquisite — and valuable — than it was before."

The duke was so pleased that he ordered the work to start at once.

The engraver began by creating a special motif of flowers and scrolls, which formed a frame around the edge of the stone. Then, in the center, he engraved the duke's name in large, elegant letters. Finally, underneath he etched the duke's coat of arms.

After several days of concentrated effort, the engraver laid down his tools and declared his task complete. The results were unbelievable. The sapphire was even more breathtaking than before. No one would ever have guessed that an unsightly flaw had once marred the precious gem. And the most amazing part of it all was that the entire design was built around the crack, which formed a basic line within the whole masterpiece. The same split that had caused the duke anguish and despair was now a source of delight and rejoicing.

The duke was so thrilled that he called the crack "a stroke of good fortune."

"If the stone hadn't gotten that awful crack," he explained, "I would never have had a design engraved on it. Now it is even more beautiful and valuable than before."

Similarly, Yosef HaTzaddik tells his brothers that what seems to them to have been a fault of theirs, a terrible mistake with tragic results, has turned into a blessing for them all. It was Hashem's plan that they sell him into bondage in order that they all be saved later from the famine. What would have happened to them if Yosef hadn't been in Egypt? How would they have found food to survive?

"Don't be upset," Yosef tells them. "It was all part of Hashem's plan. It is Hashem Who carves the design of our lives. What looks to us like an ugly scratch turns out in the end to be the beginning of a beautiful design."

VaYechi

Chesed and Emes — A Binding Oath

...וַיִּקְרָא לִבְנוֹ לְיוֹסֵף וַיֹּאמֶר לוֹ...שִׂים נָא יָדְךָ תַּחַת יְרֵכִי
וְעָשִׂיתָ עִמָּדִי חֶסֶד וֶאֱמֶת אַל נָא תִקְבְּרֵנִי בְּמִצְרָיִם.

...and [Yaakov] called his son Yosef and said to him: "...place your hand under my thigh and deal with me with love and kindness — do not bury me in Egypt."

(Bereishis 47:29)

YOSEF CERTAINLY LOVED his father deeply and always made every effort to carry out any request Yaakov made of him. Nevertheless Yaakov Avinu asked Yosef to swear not to bury him in Egypt. It seems strange that Yaakov Avinu did not rely on Yosef to fulfill his last wish without an oath. Wasn't Yosef's word good enough?

Another question: What is the meaning of the expression "kindness and truth — *chesed ve'emes*"? If taking Yaakov's body to Eretz Yisrael for burial was an act of truth, how could it have been an act of kindness at the same time? The two words, *chesed* and *emes*, seem to contradict each other. If I give someone ten dollars because he earned it, or because I owe it to him, this is an act of *emes*. Truthfulness and honesty require that I give a person his due. On the other hand, if I wish to give someone a present of ten dollars because I love him, this would be an act of *chesed*, born of a desire to give the other person pleasure.

We would think that Yosef's motivation in fulfilling Yaakov Avinu's request would be the latter one, a desire to do one last *chesed* for the father he so loved and respected. Why then does Yaakov ask Yosef to deal with him in both kindness and truth? How does truth come into the picture here?

The Dubno Maggid explains with a *mashal*:

Reuven wanted to give his dear friend David a present that would truly show how much he valued their friendship. Since Reuven himself was extremely wealthy, and dealt in real estate, he decided to present David with a beautiful new home. He could just picture himself handing the keys to his dear friend! How pleased David and his family would be! Reuven could hardly wait. It made him smile just to think how good he would feel when the big day came and he could hand David the deed to his new house.

But there was one problem Reuven had to overcome. He knew that some of his relatives wouldn't approve of his gift. They would say that he should keep the money for himself and not spend such a tremendous sum on other people. These relatives would object vigorously if they heard about Reuven's plan, and they might stop him from carrying it out.

Determined not to let that happen, Reuven asked his lawyer to draw up a bill of sale for the house he wanted to buy for David. The contract stated that Reuven would pay for the house and that it would become David's property. Then Reuven happily signed the document and presented a copy to David.

Now he was certain that no one could foil his plans; the house would surely become David's because if anyone stopped Reuven from paying for it when the time came, the courts would interfere and force him to live up to the contract he had signed. What Reuven originally wanted to do as a token of friendship, as a *chesed*, the courts would force him to do as a legal obligation, an act of *emes*. Thus, both *chesed* and *emes* played a part in Reuven's plan.

Similarly, Yaakov Avinu knew that Yosef would certainly want with all his heart to honor his request to take his body back to Eretz Yisrael for burial. But would Pharaoh agree? Yaakov was afraid he wouldn't.

Pharaoh had seen with his own eyes how the seven-year famine had stopped after only two years when Yaakov Avinu had come to Egypt. Again the waters of the Nile flowed freely and the country was blessed with an abundance of food. Pharaoh and the Egyptians didn't believe in Hashem. They didn't realize that the true source of their blessing was Hashem and not Yaakov Avinu, in whose merit Hashem had stopped the famine ahead of time. Consequently, Pharaoh would not easily be persuaded to let Yaakov's body out of Egypt. He would insist that the tzaddik be buried in Egypt and then turn his tomb into a shrine, a place of *avodah zarah!*

Yaakov Avinu had devoted his entire life to *avodas Hashem*, serving Hashem in every possible way. Even after his death, he would not allow his body to be used for something that contradicted the basic belief that every blessing and benefit comes from Hashem alone. Therefore Yaakov Avinu sought a way to force Pharaoh to allow Yosef to take his body back to Eretz Yisrael for burial.

By asking Yosef to take an oath, Yaakov knew

he would leave Pharaoh no choice but to agree. When Yosef became viceroy of Egypt, he had taken an oath to serve Pharaoh loyally. Pharaoh surely wanted Yosef to keep his word. If Pharaoh forced Yosef to disregard the oath he had taken to bury his father in Eretz Yisrael, why should Yosef feel obligated to honor the oath he had taken before Pharaoh?

Yaakov Avinu solved his problem in advance by asking Yosef to swear that he would bury him in Eretz Yisrael. That is why he asked Yosef to perform an act of both *chesed* and *emes*: *chesed* in burying him in Eretz Yisrael, and *emes* in fulfilling the pledge he had made to his beloved father.

Shemos

"In Your Name"

...ה' לָמָה הֲרֵעֹתָה לָעָם הַזֶּה לָמָה זֶּה שְׁלַחְתָּנִי. וּמֵאָז בָּאתִי
אֶל פַּרְעֹה לְדַבֵּר בִּשְׁמֶךָ הֵרַע לָעָם הַזֶּה....

*...Hashem, why have You allotted misfortune
to this people? Why did You send me? For
since I have come to Pharaoh to speak in Your
Name, he has done evil to this people....*
(Shemos 5:22-23)

WHEN HASHEM FIRST revealed Himself
to Moshe Rabbeinu, He told Moshe that
he would lead the Jewish people out of
Egypt. Hashem commanded Moshe Rabbeinu to
tell Pharaoh that He wanted the Jewish people to
go into the desert and offer sacrifices to Him. Not
only did Pharaoh refuse to allow Israel to go serve
Hashem, he even stopped supplying the Jews with
the straw they needed to make the bricks he de-

manded of them. Instead of being rescued, they were forced to work even harder — just the opposite of what Moshe Rabbeinu had hoped for.

Thus, Moshe Rabbeinu turned to Hashem and spoke the words quote above.

Moshe's comment would have made sense even without the words "in Your Name." Why then does he include them?

The Dubno Maggid answers with a *mashal*:

There were two extremely rich men in Greenstadt: Paul White and John Black. Both lived in huge mansions and had enormous staffs of servants, cooks, valets, nursemaids — whatever they could possibly want. But even so, neither man was happy. Each one wanted to be known as the richest man in town, the leader, the best and most esteemed citizen of Greenstadt, and neither could be happy without this recognition. John Black felt that if only Paul White would lose all his money, or move away, or somehow just vanish into thin air, he would be the happiest man on earth. It was only that horrible Paul White who stood in the way of his happiness in life, and he hated him with all his heart.

Paul White felt exactly the same way about John Black: he detested him through and through. No one even dared mention the name

John Black in his presence, and with good reason.

One day Paul White's servant Tom was on his way home from the market with a basketful of fresh vegetables. En route, he passed right by John Black, who decided to use the opportunity to let Paul White know what he thought of him. As Tom walked by, Black gave him a powerful shove with both hands and sent him tumbling. Apples and tomatoes rolled about in all directions as the unfortunate servant lay in the mud, holding his shoulder and moaning.

But it was not only Tom's shoulder that ached. His pride was hurt, too. "Do you know who I am?" he yelled up at John Black. "I work for Mr. Paul White. He's the richest, most powerful fellow in town. Just wait till he hears about this. He'll really get even with you!"

Nothing could have angered John Black more. "Richest man in town?! Most powerful?!" Now he'd *really* show this miserable fellow who was in charge in Greenstadt. With that, he fell on poor Tom and battered him black and blue.

Some friends helped Tom get home and into bed. Later, when he went back to work, he didn't say anything to his boss. But the cuts and bruises spoke for themselves.

"What happened?" White asked in alarm. "How did you get that black eye?"

Tom told White his story.

"Maybe he didn't know you work for me," said Paul White.

Now Tom saw his chance. He wanted to get Paul White so furious with John Black that he would punish him for what he'd done. And he knew how to do it.

"Didn't know?!" he exclaimed. "Of course he knew! I myself warned him when he first started up with me. I told him that I worked for you and that he had better watch his step, because you'd pay him back tit for tat. But when I mentioned your name, not only didn't he stop, but he started hitting me even harder."

That was all White needed to hear. Clearly, Black bore no personal grudge against Tom; his anger was directed against White himself, and Tom was just an innocent pawn in the long, drawn-out battle between the two rivals.

White grew pale with fury.

"Just wait," he thundered, "and you'll see what I'll do to him for this!"

Paul White kept his word. He cleverly laid a trap for John Black and got his revenge sevenfold.

Moshe Rabbeinu knew that the Jews lacked the merit needed for Hashem to intervene on their behalf and save them from Pharaoh's cruel decrees. But Moshe Rabbeinu was such a faithful leader and protector of Israel that he loved his people even more than himself. If the Jews did not have enough mitzvos to be redeemed in their own merit, Moshe Rabbeinu was determined to find a way to rescue them from their suffering.

Therefore, Moshe Rabbeinu stressed that he had spoken to Pharaoh "in Your Name," in the Name of Hashem, as if to say: "Even if we, the people of Israel, don't deserve to be saved, take us out of Egypt for the sake of Your Name, to protect Your honor."

And Hashem answered him accordingly: "Now you will see what I will do to Pharaoh, for with a strong hand he shall send them forth and with a strong hand he shall drive them out of his land" (Shemos 6:1).

VaEira

Show Me Proof

כִּי יְדַבֵּר אֲלֵכֶם פַּרְעֹה לֵאמֹר תְּנוּ לָכֶם מוֹפֵת וְאָמַרְתָּ אֶל אַהֲרֹן קַח אֶת מַטְּךָ וְהַשְׁלֵךְ לִפְנֵי פַרְעֹה יְהִי לְתַנִּין.

When Pharaoh will speak to you, saying, "Show a wonder for yourselves," say to Aharon: "Take your staff and cast it down before Pharaoh — it will become a serpent."

(Shemos 7:9)

WHEN HASHEM COMMANDED Moshe and Aharon to demand that Pharaoh send the Jewish people out of Egypt, He warned them that Pharaoh might ask for a sign to prove that it really was Hashem Who had sent them.

Chazal discuss whether Pharaoh was justified in asking for a sign. According to at least one opinion, he was. The Dubno Maggid explains why with a *mashal*:

Daniel had worked in Reb Simchah's business for years. Everyone knew that he was Reb Simchah's right-hand man and could be trusted anywhere, anytime, with any job.

Reb Simchah had a close friend, Reb Monish, who was very wealthy. Whenever Reb Simchah needed some extra cash on hand to close a business deal during the course of the day, he would send the faithful Daniel over to Reb Monish's office to ask for a loan. Reb Monish knew Daniel almost as well as he knew Reb Simchah himself, and was always glad to oblige with the funds needed. Like Reb Simchah, Reb Monish relied on Daniel completely.

Once Daniel left town for several weeks to attend a family wedding. It was difficult for Reb Simchah to manage without him so he hired a young man to help with whatever errands he could. Avraham, the new boy, was a quick learner and did his best to be of assistance.

One day, Reb Simchah called Avraham and said, "Go to Reb Monish and ask him to lend me four hundred crowns. Tell him I'll pay him back, *be'ezras Hashem,* by the end of the week."

Avraham went straight to Reb Monish's office

and asked to speak to the owner himself.

"I'm the owner," said a tall figure sitting at a desk full of letters, bills, and official-looking documents. "What can I do for you?"

"Reb Simchah sent me to ask for a loan of four hundred crowns. He said he will be able to repay it, *be'ezras Hashem*, by the end of the week."

Reb Monish looked at Avraham in surprise. Who was he? Where was Daniel? Was this young boy trying to trick him out of four hundred crowns or had Reb Simchah sent him? He couldn't insult Avraham by telling him that he suspected him of lying, but he knew it would be foolish to believe every stranger who walked into his office and asked for a loan.

Reb Monish knew what to do without hurting anyone's feelings.

"Could I see the *shtar* [promissory note]?" he asked.

"The *shtar*? I don't have a shtar. Reb Simchah didn't say anything about a *shtar*. He didn't give me one."

"Perhaps he forgot," said Reb Monish. "Better go back and ask him for it."

Avraham did as he was told.

"A *shtar*?" Reb Simchah's eyebrows rose in disbelief. "What happened? Reb Monish never asks me for a shtar. I have to hear this for myself."

Buttoning up his coat, Reb Simchah headed straight for his friend's place of business.

"Reb Monish! What happened?" Reb Simchah accosted his friend. "Why is this time different from all the other times you gave me loans? You've never asked for a *shtar* before. Did I do something wrong that you don't trust me anymore?"

"Reb Simchah! Don't be upset," Reb Monish calmed his friend. "Of course I trust you. Nothing's changed about you — I know *you*. But I don't know your new worker, the young fellow who asked for the four hundred crowns a few minutes ago. I don't recall ever seeing him before, and I certainly have no reason to believe him when he says that you sent him and that you will be responsible for the money. When Daniel comes, I *know* that he works for you, but this fellow? I have no way of knowing who sent him. That's why I asked for a *shtar*."

"I see," said Reb Simchah. "Now I understand. Of course, you were quite right to ask for a *shtar*. It was the only sensible thing to do."

When Moshe Rabbeinu and Aharon HaKohen first appeared before Pharaoh, they told him that Hashem had sent them: "...and they said to Pharaoh: 'So said Hashem, the God of Israel: Send forth My people...' " (Shemos 5:1).

But Pharaoh replied: "Who is Hashem that I should listen to His voice and send Israel forth? I don't know Hashem, nor will I let Israel go" (5:2).

The Midrash tells us that Pharaoh had a directory of all the nations of the world and all the idols they served. Of course, Pharaoh's list didn't include the Name of Hashem, *lehavdil*. It contained only the names of idols made by human beings, statues formed out of stone or wood to serve as national gods. What would the Name of Hashem — *lehavdil* — be doing in a list of sticks and stones?

Therefore Pharaoh answered: "*Who is Hashem?* I never heard of Him. He's not on my list of idols, so *I won't let Israel go.*"

Pharaoh needed a sign, a proof that Hashem did indeed control the whole world. That's why Hashem told Moshe Rabbeinu and Aharon:

"When Pharaoh will speak to you, saying, 'Show a wonder for yourselves,' say to Aharon, 'Take your staff and cast it down before Pharaoh — it will become a serpent' " (7:9).

Bo

He is First

הַחֹדֶשׁ הַזֶּה לָכֶם רֹאשׁ חֳדָשִׁים....

This month shall be for you the first of months...

(Shemos 12:2)

THE TORAH CALLS Nissan *rishon*, the *first* month. The Midrash lists several other things described as "first": Hashem, Zion, the Beis HaMikdash, Mashiach, and Eisav.

What do all these have in common? The Midrash explains: Hashem, Who is called *rishon*, will come and build the Beis HaMikdash, which is called *rishon*, and will punish Eisav, who is called *rishon*. Then the Mashiach, who is called *rishon*, will come. And all this will happen in the month of Nissan, which is also called *rishon*.

Nowadays there are people and groups and

even entire nations that speak foolishly or
wickedly and say, "Who is Hashem? Why should
I fear Him or do as He commands? Why not enjoy
myself while I can?" Such people belong to the
group David HaMelech described thousands of
years ago: "...the fool says in his heart, 'There is
no God'..." (Tehillim 14:1).

In the future — may it be very soon — Hashem
will show everyone that He is the *rishon*, the first
in command. How? The Dubno Maggid explains
with a *mashal*:

Two poor fellows decided to keep each other
company as they wandered from one town to
another. One was a tall, well-built fellow, hale and
hearty, who looked as though he'd never been sick
— or even tired — a day in his life. Bristling with
energy, he had little patience for his companion,
who looked as though he'd never seen a well day
in his life. His skin festered with sores, his limbs
ached when he moved, and his insides rebelled
when he ate anything but the lightest of foods.
Misery and pain were his lot, and his suffering
was none the lighter for the scorn his robust
friend heaped upon him as they trudged over hill
and dale.

"Never seen such a sickly chap in my life! At
the rate you're crawling along, it will be spring
before we reach Leipzig!"

Beset with so many aches and pains, the poor fellow held his tongue. But in his heart he prayed: "O God, see how I am suffering and how this heartless fellow insults me and puts me to shame again and again. Please, God, let me see the day when he will suffer just because he *is* so strong and healthy, and I, in contrast, will benefit and be happy because of all my illness and pain."

To us it might seem a strange request. How could anyone be made to regret his good health and strong muscles? Even stranger: how could sores and disease become a blessing? It seems impossible.

But as it happened, that very week the king's chief of staff dropped dead. A giant of a fellow, "Geoffrey the Giant" had planted terror in the hearts of his enemies. Bare-handed, he had up-rooted trees and slung them against city gates like a battering ram. He had caught boulders cata-pulted against the castle walls and tossed them back at the enemy. Where would the king find a replacement for such a legendary warrior?

Then came a second blow only three days later: the court physician also died. He, too, had to be replaced. But again, the king worried, where would he find someone with such extraordinary skill and knowledge?

A search was made throughout the land, and

a few weeks later there were candidates for both positions.

The king singled out one huge soldier and decided to test him.

"How can you prove that you will be as valiant in battle as Geoffrey, who used to send our enemies fleeing in fright?"

"Let the king find a big, healthy fellow, hale and hearty, and just let me have a few minutes with him. I'll finish him off with one finger!" bragged the bully.

The king then turned to the doctor who had been suggested as the new court physician. "And what about you? How can you prove yourself to me?"

"Your Majesty," replied the doctor, "let your runners seek the most diseased subject in the kingdom, someone plagued with a myriad of illnesses; just give me a chance, and I will cure all his ills, one after the other."

"So be it!" replied the king. "We will give each of you the trial you have requested. If you succeed," he said to each in turn, "you will head my troops, and you will serve as my physician."

So again he sent his runners to search, this time for a tall, strapping fellow to test the warrior's strength, and a sickly weakling — afflicted with as many diseases as possible — to test the doctor's powers of healing.

Not only did the king's officers find just the two people they needed, but they found them together, in one stroke. The two traveling companions, one the picture of health, the other ailing from head to toe, had hardly entered the city gates when they caught the eye of the king's guard.

"Hey, you two! Stop a minute! Wait right where you are!"

Startled and frightened, the two did as they were told.

"Come with me," ordered the guard.

They were taken to a royal coach and told to climb in.

"Take them to the palace at once," the guard instructed the coachman. "And tell the officer of the day to call off the search."

The sickly gentleman had a hard time controlling his anxiety. Here he was, riddled with illness and uncertainty, and on top of it all he had to endure his companion's endless taunts. Even now, on the way to the royal palace — and maybe to the dungeon, or even worse — the fellow didn't stop bragging about his strength and prowess.

"They probably want me to join the king's cavalry, or become a watchman at the palace. They could see at a glance what a hardy, healthy soldier I'd make. Now you're going to see royalty, just because you're with me. I'll bet you never

The two traveling companions, one the picture of health, the other ailing from head to toe, had hardly entered the city gates when they caught the eye of the king's guard.

thought an old bag of bones like you would be paying his respects to His Royal Highness, eh?" And with that he gave his terror-stricken friend a jab in the ribs, doubling him over in pain.

As the coach drew up to the royal gates, the poor fellow could only pray silently: "Dear God, just let me come out of here alive!"

The two men were ushered into the throne room without delay. The strong man was so pleased with himself and his apparent good fortune that his chest puffed up with pride.

The king took a good look at him, turned to a servant, and declared, "He will do."

By now, the cocky fellow wouldn't have been surprised if the king had knighted him on the spot. But the king's intentions were, in fact, far different. The giant warrior was called in and, good to his word, he finished off the braggart with hardly more than a wave of his hand.

Next the king turned his attention to the sickly fellow, by now faint with dread at the fate he assumed awaited him. He hardly heard the king call out: "Take this pitiful knave to the physician, and report to me on his progress!"

Under the doctor's expert care, the fellow became a picture of health. His sores were healed, he gained an appetite, and he put on weight. The physician managed to cure his every ailment, enabling him to live a full, healthy life.

In the future, Hashem will make things happen in such an "unnatural" manner that they will defy any natural explanation. He will raise up to power and greatness those who are lowly, like the poor, sickly man, and bring low those who appear strong and who arrogantly use their power to oppress others — like the healthy pauper who couldn't stop bragging and making fun of his suffering companion. The day will come when Hashem will take the nation that rules the world and suddenly crush its power until it is as insignificant as the dust of the earth. That will be one sign that Hashem is *rishon* — the Cause of everything that happens.

But there will be a another sign: Hashem will take the nation that has always been at the mercy of others, that has suffered endlessly and been rejected and hated by all, and suddenly make it mighty. Everyone will seek to befriend it and be proud to serve it.

This is the meaning of the Midrash: In Nissan, the first of months, Hashem — the first Cause of all that happens — will send us Mashiach, who is called "first." He will punish Eisav, who was born first, before Yaakov, and make him like the dust of the earth.

Then He will build the Beis HaMikdash, also described as "first." As a result, the entire world will at last clearly see that it is Hashem and only Hashem Who is First, Who controls our lives and makes everything happen according to His plan. "...on that day, Hashem will be One and His Name will be One" (Zechariah 14:9).

BeShalach
The Importance of a Single Mitzvah

וַיֹּאמֶר ה׳ אֶל מֹשֶׁה מַה תִּצְעַק אֵלָי דַּבֵּר אֶל בְּנֵי יִשְׂרָאֵל
וְיִסָּעוּ.

*And Hashem said to Moshe, "Why are you
crying out to Me? Speak to the Israelites and
let them start moving!"*

(Shemos 14:15)

BNEI YISRAEL HAD slaughtered the *korban
Pesach* as Hashem had commanded. They
had borrowed riches from their Egyptian
neighbors as Hashem had commanded. Now they
had followed Moshe Rabbeinu into the desert, as
Hashem had commanded. They were waiting to
see the miracles Hashem had promised to perform
for them when He rescued them from Egypt.

But Pharaoh and his men were chasing them,
and there was nowhere to flee except into the

waves of the sea before them. So Moshe Rabbeinu cried out to Hashem that He save the Jewish people.

Hashem's answer? "Now is no time for prayer; tell the people to go forward into the sea and it will split for them."

Usually Chazal tell us that prayer is the right way to respond to distress; what was different here?

The Dubno Maggid explains with a *mashal*:

Lord Whitehall was extremely wealthy; his estate was said to be worth millions. Yet Whitehall's son, Edward, had no idea how to earn a penny. He was a fragile, only child, and his father had always sheltered him from the wear and tear of even his minor financial dealings, much less the management of an entire estate.

However, as Edward grew older, his father realized that life would have to change one day for the lad. He weighed the various alternatives, and then came to a decision:

"If I wait until Edward marries and then tell him he must worry about earning his own livelihood, it will be unfair. He won't even know how to support himself, much less a wife and children. He must start some sort of business now so he can gradually learn the ways of the world."

Lord Whitehall summoned Edward and told him his plan: "Each week I want you to earn six crowns by yourself. On Friday you'll come to me with your six crowns and I'll give you another twenty-four so you'll have enough to live on. But remember — I won't give you even a penny until you've earned the full six crowns that week."

Edward agreed, and the plan went into action. Each Friday the son brought his father six crowns, and Whitehall added another twenty-four.

Then one week Edward earned nearly the entire six crowns by Tuesday. He was lacking only one more penny. "Never mind," he thought. "What difference will it make to my father, who has millions of crowns?"

The rest of the week Edward didn't even try to earn more, for he was sure that one penny wouldn't matter.

But when Friday came, Edward found out that he had made a big mistake.

"Count your money again, Edward," said Lord Whitehall, thinking Edward had erred in tallying his profits. "You don't have a full six crowns here."

"Yes, I know, my lord," answered Edward. "But it's only one penny short. What difference does one little penny make to a millionaire like you?"

"That one penny of yours is very significant to

me. In fact, it means more to me than the twenty-four crowns I want to give you now but can't. I have so much gold and silver in my treasury that twenty-four crowns — or ten times that amount — is all the same to me. The coins are just sitting here not being used, anyway. It's no more effort for me to count out two one-hundred-crown pieces than two ten-crown pieces. I don't have to *earn* the money; I only have to count it out and give it to you.

"But it's different with the six crowns you agreed to bring me each week. That isn't money you have sitting in your strongbox. That is money you earn. Each additional penny means an additional effort, so every little coin counts. It shows me how much you tried this week to earn your own living.

"We have an agreement and I expect you to keep it: First, you earn six crowns; then, I provide the rest. Every penny of those six crowns is important to me, and I cannot let you have the rest of your thirty-crown allowance until you have earned every bit of your share: six crowns, and not a penny less!"

Hashem was just waiting to save the Jews through miracles and wonders. But first they had to earn His special protection by carrying out every one of His orders. They had brought the *korban Pesach* as Hashem had commanded them. Then they had prepared to leave Egypt, as they had been told by Hashem. Every step that each Jewish man, woman, and child took out of Egypt was dear to Hashem.

When the Jews reached the shores of the Red Sea, they thought there was nothing more they could do; now it was up to Hashem to save them. But no: Hashem required a few more steps from them — right into the waters of the sea itself. So He told Moshe Rabbeinu not to pray for a miracle now, but to take the last few steps needed to earn their miraculous rescue from Pharaoh and his men.

Once they had fully "earned" it, Hashem showed them greater wonders than any human being had ever seen: "Hashem saved Israel that day, from the hand of Egypt.... And Israel saw the great hand that Hashem wielded in Egypt..." (Shemos 14:30-31).

Yisro

"Ashreinu"

וַיֹּאמֶר ה' אֶל מֹשֶׁה כֹּה תֹאמַר אֶל בְּנֵי יִשְׂרָאֵל אַתֶּם רְאִיתֶם
כִּי מִן הַשָּׁמַיִם דִּבַּרְתִּי עִמָּכֶם.

*And Hashem said to Moshe, "Thus shall you
say to the children of Israel: 'You have seen
that I have spoken with you from heaven.' "*
(Shemos 20:19)

WHEN MOSHE RABBEINU went up to receive the Torah for the Jewish people, the angels objected to Hashem: "Why give Your precious Torah to mere human beings?" They wanted to keep the Torah in *shamayim*, where they felt it belonged.

At first glance, the angels' attitude seems very strange. The Midrash tells us that the reason Hashem created the world in the first place was so that the Jews could eventually receive the

Torah on Har Sinai, study it day and night, and observe its mitzvos.

If so, why did the angels protest? Did they really think they could convince Hashem to change His reason for creating the world?

The Dubno Maggid gives us the answer with one of his *meshalim*:

The beloved *melamed* of Zelstadt was getting on in years. For as long as most people in town could remember, Reb Chaim Reit had taught the little cheder boys their *aleph-beis*, and they all loved him dearly. Gently but firmly, Reb Chaim had gotten even the liveliest of children to sit quietly and learn *Chumash*. He was also widely respected as a *talmid chacham*, and even the most learned members of Zelstadt's *kehillah* would gather to hear Reb Chaim's weekly *parashah shiur*.

But as Reb Chaim grew older, he felt the time had come to slow down somewhat. He didn't want to stop teaching completely, so he hit upon an idea: he and his wife would move to a small town with a smaller cheder; there, life would be quieter.

Reb Chaim's wife also liked the idea, so Reb Chaim wrote to nearby Frischdorf and asked whether the town would like to hire him as a *melamed*. The answer came back right away:

Frischdorf would be delighted to have the famous *melamed* teach its children.

The little town of Frischdorf was alive with excitement. It wasn't every day that a *talmid chacham* of Reb Chaim Reit's caliber joined its ranks. Both the town's wagon drivers had scrubbed and polished their carts. One cart would be for Reb Chaim and his wife, and the dignitaries who had been chosen to accompany the new *melamed* back to Frischdorf. The second cart would bring Reb Chaim's belongings. With hearty cheers and farewells, the delegation left Frischdorf for Zelstadt.

Reb Chaim welcomed them warmly. But as he was shaking hands with the Frischdorfers, three of Zelstadt's leading personalities rushed up to him and exclaimed: "Rebbe! Reb Chaim! You're not really going to leave us, are you? What will we do without you? Who will teach our little children? Who will explain the *parashah* to us on Shabbos?"

Reb Chaim was both surprised and very moved. What could he say?

"But I discussed it with you two weeks ago. Don't you remember? You all agreed that I was free to do what I felt was best for my wife and me. And, as I told you then, we feel it would be better for us to move to Frischdorf."

"Ah, Rebbe, if that's how it is — if it's better for

But the drivers wasted no time. They were strong, hefty men, and they had no intention of putting up with behavior like this.

you — we won't press you to stay. We'll miss you, but we want you to do what is best for you."

Relieved that everything was straightened out, Reb Chaim signaled the porters to load his crates and bundles onto the wagons. The porters heaved and hauled, arranged and rearranged, tucked a blanket in here and a pot in there, and finished off by tying everything up with a stout rope. But just as they were ready to set off, four local residents dashed up to the drivers and started pulling them away from their carts and unhitching the horses.

"You can't take Reb Chaim from us!" the four shouted. "He's ours! He's our rebbe! We refuse. Leave him here!"

Poor Reb Chaim. Again he was at a loss for words. But the drivers wasted no time. They were strong, hefty men, and they had no intention of putting up with behavior like this. Grabbing one fellow by the arm and another by his collar, they dragged the protestors off to the rabbi of Zelstadt. Let *him* decide what to do!

The rabbi listened to the drivers' story and then asked the protestors to explain themselves.

"It's quite simple," answered the men. "When Reb Chaim first decided to move, he asked whether we would agree to his leaving Zelstadt. We told him that we would miss him if he decided to leave, but that he should do what would be best for him and his wife."

"But even so, you tried to stop him from leaving town today?" asked the rabbi.

"Of course," replied the men. "We can't let Frischdorf just walk away with our Reb Chaim. Why, if we don't protest, they'll think that we don't even mind. They'll think that Reb Chaim is just another fine Jew who's moved into town. How will they know about his unmatched *yiras shamayim* and his wonderful *shiurim*? They'll never ask him *kashes*; they'll never know what a *talmid chacham* he is. We want them to appreciate him and give him the respect he deserves, so we decided to show them how much we would really like him to stay."

The *malachim* knew that the Torah was intended for the Jewish people and not for angels. They knew they would eventually have to let Moshe Rabbeinu take it from them. But they wanted to be certain that we human beings would appreciate it fully. That's why they protested. Otherwise, people might have said, "If Torah is so wonderful, why did the angels give it up and let Moshe Rabbeinu take it down to earth?"

Now that we know how much the *malachim*

coveted the Torah and wanted it to stay in their midst, we realize what a gift Hashem gave us on Har Sinai.

Ashreinu mah tov chelkeinu — how happy are we, for how goodly is our portion: the holy Torah.

Mishpatim

Hashem, Co-Signer of Our Loans

אִם כֶּסֶף תַּלְוֶה אֶת עַמִּי אֶת הֶעָנִי עִמָּךְ לֹא תִהְיֶה לוֹ כְּנֹשֶׁה....

If you lend money to My people, to the poor with you, you shall not be to [them] as a creditor....

(Shemos 22:24)

THE MIDRASH EXPLAINS this verse by quoting another one: "One who gives graciously to the poor lends to God, and He pays him his reward" (Mishlei 19:17).

But how can one be said to be lending to the Master of the Universe? The Dubno Maggid offers a *mashal*:

Shimon needed a loan. Reuven readily consented to provide one, but he asked Shimon to find two people to co-sign the *shtar* (promissory note). That way, if Shimon was unable to repay the loan when the time came, Reuven could turn to the co-signers and ask *them* to return his money.

Shimon set out to find two friends who would co-sign for the loan. Aryeh, a well-to-do and good-natured fellow, said "yes" straight away, but it was hard for Shimon to think of anyone else who would be able to sign for him.

Shimon needed the money very much, so he decided to approach his close friend Binyamin Levy, even though Binyamin had hardly a penny to his name.

When Binyamin agreed, everything was set. Shimon happily returned to Reuven and presented the *shtar* bearing the signatures of his two guarantors, Aryeh and Binyamin. Reuven handed Shimon the sum he needed, and filed the *shtar* away with the rest of his papers in his desk.

Shimon was determined to make the most of his borrowed funds. He heard about a huge fair to be held in the capital. It would take him two weeks to get there, but people assured him it would be time well spent. So he hired a driver and was on his way.

Once there, he threw himself into trading day and night. Hashem was with him, and he doubled his investment again and again.

With all the excitement and calculations about

what merchandise to buy, Shimon forgot that in a few days the loan would be due. Who would pay Reuven back his money?

Meanwhile, back home Reuven sat at his desk, Shimon's *shtar* in his hand. He checked the date again. No, there was no mistake. The loan had been due on *rosh chodesh.* Today was the fifth. Five days had gone by and there was still no sign of Shimon. Nor of Reuven's money.

"Yitzchak!" Reuven called out to one of his clerks. "Yitzchak, take a look at this *shtar.* It's overdue. I want you to go find out what's happened to Shimon."

It didn't take long for Yitzchak to come back with the news. Shimon had left town right after he'd received the funds from Reuven. No one knew where he was or when he would return, not even his wife and family.

"Good thing I insisted that the *shtar* be co-signed," said Reuven. "Have a look who the guarantors are, Yitzchak, and let them know what happened. I'd like my money back!"

"There are two names here, Reb Reuven: Aryeh and Binyamin. Which one should I go to?"

"I don't know either fellow. Go into town and see what you can find out about both of them," Reuven instructed Yitzchak. "Then we'll decide whom to ask for the money."

Once in town, Yitzchak started asking around.

"Yes, I know Aryeh. He lives two streets over from here, in that big, green house — three stories, his place is. Largest house on the block. You can't miss it. That was his coach that just went by — the maroon one with the fancy gilt around the windows. And those horses — did you see how they pranced along, all fine and dandy? He was headed for home, so you'll probably find him in now. Just turn right at the corner and follow your nose. Ask anybody — they all know Aryeh."

It wasn't so easy to find out about Binyamin. People didn't seem to recognize the name straight away.

After several inquiries, someone directed Yitzchak to a part of town quite different from Aryeh's district. The streets were narrow, the road muddy, and the buildings more like shacks than homes.

Yitzchak wondered what would happen here in a storm. He could picture the street full of shingles and shutters torn off by the wind and scattered along the length of the street. Did he really have the right address? How could anyone who lived in such a tumbledown area afford to repay a major loan for a friend?

Yitzchak asked a passerby for further directions.

The man's hat was battered and torn on one side, his coat had several patches. He seemed to fit into the neighborhood; maybe he would know something about this Binyamin who had signed the *shtar*.

"Hey, Reb Yid," Yitzchak stopped him. "Know anyone around here called Binyamin?"

"Binyamin?" the fellow echoed. "Sure, I'm Binyamin. What can I do for you?"

Yitzchak was startled but decided to make sure. "You're Binyamin? And you know a fellow called Shimon? Borrowed some money a few weeks ago and then left town on business?"

"Sure, I'm the one you're looking for. What's wrong? Why are you so surprised?"

"Well...." Yitzchak didn't know what to say. How could he tell someone who barely had clothes on his back that he wanted him to pay back someone else's loan? Who knew whether this Binyamin and his family had even eaten anything that day?

Back in the office, Yitzchak reported his findings to his employer, Reuven.

"Hmm...so that's the story. Well, there's surely no point in asking Binyamin to pay me back. The only sensible thing to do is to ask Reb Aryeh to repay the debt in full. If he's such a well-to-do fellow, Shimon's debt will hardly make a difference to him one way or the other. He'll probably pay it back without a second thought."

The next day, Yitzchak approached Reb Aryeh with the *shtar* and received the full amount on the spot, just as Reuven had predicted.

Yitzchak returned to the office all smiles. "Look, he paid everything! Now I'm so glad I didn't ask Binyamin for any of the money. He wouldn't have been able to give it to me, anyway, so why cause him the embarrassment and pain of saying, 'I haven't got it'? In the end, we got the full amount back in any case. Why hurt someone for nothing?"

The way of the world is to lend money in order to earn money. John lends Paul $100 on condition that Paul pay back $100 plus another $10 in interest. That way, John earns $10 for every $100 he lends out. It's John's way of making a living.

And when Paul borrows the money, he must sign a contract stating when he will pay back the $110. If he misses that date and pays only later, he will have to pay John more than $10 extra. There will probably be a fine to pay, or additional interest. If Paul is more than a day or two late, he can be sure that John will be looking for him and waiting impatiently for his money back.

That is the way of the world.

But, *lehavdil*, within *klal Yisrael*, it is just the opposite. The Torah commands us not to charge interest. It is as though all of *klal Yisrael* has one big loan fund. Those who have extra money put cash into the fund, and those who need it may borrow what they require. From time to time, each person's situation changes. Sometimes I lend, sometimes I borrow, depending on my circumstances. But we all have an agreement — a mitzvah — not to collect interest from each other. *Klal Yisrael*'s general fund is there to lend a helping hand to fellow Jews, not to serve as a way of making a living.

We are also taught to avoid embarrassing someone who owes us money but can't pay us back right now. Not only shouldn't we press such a person to make payment, but we mustn't even mention the debt to him, or even go where we know we'll meet him, because then he'll feel shame and quiver in fright, thinking: "Oh, no! Now Chaim is going to ask me for his money back, and I'll have to admit that I don't have it."

This is the lesson of the verse in Mishlei: "One who gives graciously to the poor lends to God, and He pays him his reward." The poor man accepts our *tzedakah* as a *gift*, but Hashem views it as a *loan*, which He repays sevenfold.

Therefore, when a poor person can't repay a loan, we should do as Reuven did in the Maggid's *mashal*: we should look to our wealthy Co-Signer, Who has all the riches in the world, and Who has blessed us with the resources needed to perform His mitzvos.

Ki Sisa

The Healer of the Living

וַיָּשָׁב מֹשֶׁה אֶל ה׳ וַיֹּאמַר אָנָּא חָטָא הָעָם הַזֶּה חֲטָאָה גְדֹלָה
וַיַּעֲשׂוּ לָהֶם אֱלֹהֵי זָהָב.

*And Moshe returned to Hashem and said, "Oh,
this people has committed a great sin, and
they have made gods of gold for themselves."*
(Shemos 32:31)

AM YISRAEL HAD sinned very gravely. Only forty days after receiving the Torah on Har Sinai, the Jews had made a golden calf and worshipped it. So serious was their *aveirah* that Hashem was ready to destroy the entire nation — except for Moshe Rabbeinu, from whom He would build a new people.

Moshe Rabbeinu, the faithful shepherd of his people, wanted above all to prevent the destruction of *bnei Yisrael*. Just as he had pleaded with Hashem to rescue Israel from the hands of Pharaoh, now Moshe Rabbeinu davened to Hashem to have mercy on the Jews and not destroy them.

But Moshe Rabbeinu's words seem at first very strange. We would have expected him to try to make the sin seem less serious than it was, not more so. Why then did Moshe Rabbeinu say, "...this people has committed a great sin..."?

The Dubno Maggid explains with a *mashal*:

Chaim and Meir were two beggars who became fast friends. Together they trudged from one town to the next, knocked on doors, and asked for a bite to eat and a place to sleep.

Meir was a strong, healthy fellow whom people liked to help. But Chaim was a sorry sight. Sometimes it was all he could do to put one foot in front of the other and drag his hunched-up body to the doorstep.

People were not so anxious to welcome someone sick into their homes, so Meir was always urging Chaim to pull himself up straight and try to hide his aches and pains with a smile.

"Don't let them see how bad you feel," Meir would say to Chaim day after day, in town after town.

It certainly wasn't easy pretending that he was

fine, and the sickly Chaim bemoaned his fate to his loyal friend Meir. But there was nothing Meir could do for him except wish him a *refuah sheleimah.*

One afternoon it was getting late and the two friends were still far from the next Jewish town. Soon it would be dark, so they had no choice but to stop at a Jewish inn at the crossroads. They planned to spend the night there and continue on their way the next morning.

"Now remember," Meir whispered to his weary friend, "try to seem healthy. If the innkeeper doesn't like the looks of you, we'll have to spend the night out in a field!"

Chaim pulled himself up as tall as he could and managed a wan smile.

The innkeeper barely gave them a second look, and soon they were both seated at a table and enjoying a bowl of steaming soup. While Chaim tried to make himself as inconspicuous as possible, Meir took a good look at all the others spending the night at the inn. His gaze passed from one guest to the other, and all the while he reported to Chaim, who was careful not to look up from his bowl.

"There's a Jew who looks as though he's headed for the fair in Leipzig, and that little fellow next to him must be his partner. Over there at the table in the corner, there's an important-looking Jew — maybe a *rav* or a *dayan* — and next to him is — what luck! Chaim! Next to him is none other than Professor Ginzberg, the famous royal physician.

"Chaim, now's your chance! Now you can moan and groan all you want. I'm always telling you to stand straight and try to smile, but now, let's let him see how sick you are. Now, instead of hiding your aches and pains, tell him about each one of them. Don't leave anything out. The more you tell him about what hurts you, the better the chances that he can, *be'ezras Hashem*, make you well!"

Moshe Rabbeinu was asking not for forgiveness, but for a cure: "Look how ill Your people are; they have committed a very grave sin, and their *neshamah* has become very sick. Only You, Hashem, can heal them. So please make them well and righteous again."

Moshe Rabbeinu saw his people's *aveiros* not as a crime to be punished, but as an illness to be cured. Therefore, he turned to the *Rofeh Kol Chai*, Hashem, Who cures all living things, and described the "patient's" illness, just as Meir told his friend Chaim to do when they saw the famous doctor.

Hashem, the Healer, answered that He would not destroy the nation. Rather, Moshe Rabbeinu would continue to lead the Jews — and heal them — in the future.

VaYakhel

Remember Shabbos

שֵׁשֶׁת יָמִים תֵּעָשֶׂה מְלָאכָה וּבַיּוֹם הַשְּׁבִיעִי יִהְיֶה לָכֶם קֹדֶשׁ
שַׁבַּת שַׁבָּתוֹן לַה׳....

Six days work shall be done, but on the seventh day it shall be holy for you, a Shabbos of rest for Hashem....

(Shemos 35:2)

HOW CAN SHABBOS be both "for you" — for the Jewish people — and "for Hashem"? The Dubno Maggid explains with a *mashal*:

The doctors had ordered Yehudah to spend several months, or perhaps even a full year, in a warmer climate. Rosenstadt, where Yehudah lived, was known for its long, harsh winters, and the doctors feared another bout of pneumonia. As much as Yehudah wanted to stay home, he knew there was no choice. So, with a heavy heart, Yehudah took leave of his dear wife and children, and all his aunts, uncles, cousins, and close friends, and set out for sunny Glennsdorf, a health resort famous for its warm breezes.

He obtained a room in a comfortable boarding house and decided to make the best of things. He tried to keep himself busy so he wouldn't be lonely, but the days passed slowly and he longed for his home and family.

"I can't go home," thought Yehudah to himself, "but maybe I'll meet someone from Rosenstadt and hear some news of my family and friends."

Every day he took long walks, as the doctors had instructed him to do, and every day he searched the passersby — the villagers, the ped- dlers, the passengers on every passing wagon — looking for a familiar face. But day after day, only strange faces greeted Yehudah on his walks.

One *erev Shabbos*, as Yehudah was eating breakfast with the rest of the boarders, someone knocked at the door. Curious to see who was there, Yehudah peered down the hallway and caught a glimpse of a ragged figure. Something about the fellow made Yehudah pause and look again. Could it be? He stepped closer to make sure. Yes! It was none other than Chaim, the beggar from Rosenstadt! Yehudah's prayers were

So, with a heavy heart, Yehudah took leave of his dear wife and children....

answered, and he rushed to welcome the startled Chaim like a long-lost brother.

"Come in, Chaim! What brings you here? How wonderful to see you! Come have breakfast with me. I'll pay for you; you must come in and tell me the news."

Once Yehudah had Chaim comfortably seated near him at the table, with a tempting meal before him, he started plying him with questions.

"Have you seen my wife and children recently? How are they? What does the *melamed* say of my Yankele? Have the boys grown? Is it a very bad winter? When did it snow? Is there enough flour in town? Was the river frozen over yet when you left?"

Yehudah couldn't stop asking questions, and poor Chaim couldn't start eating.

"Reb Yehudah," the hungry Chaim said at last, "I know you're starved for news of home. But I'm starved, too. Just let me have a few bites of this luscious roll and a few sips of this steaming coffee, and then, *be'ezras Hashem*, I'll answer your queries."

Reb Yehudah agreed. He let Chaim eat and drink his fill. Only then did he start questioning him again.

At first, Chaim answered at length, but as he grew impatient, his answers became shorter and his glances at the grandfather clock more frequent. Chaim wanted to go.

"What's the rush?" asked Yehudah. "I've been away so long. I want to hear everything. Who knows when I'll get a chance like this again?"

"I understand, Reb Yehudah. It must be hard for you. But please understand me, too. I have only this one *erev Shabbos* in Glennsdorf and I'm afraid I won't have time to approach all the wealthy families here. Please let me go."

"How much do you think you will make if you leave right now?" asked Yehudah.

"Oh, two, maybe three gold crowns. So you see, it's nothing to sneeze at."

"I'll tell you what," proposed Yehudah. "You forget about those *gevirim*. Spend Shabbos here with me, and I'll give you three gold crowns, plus a comfortable bed, a warm room, and three luscious Shabbos *seudos* — all you can eat! It's worth it to me to hear news of home and to be able to ask you all the questions I want."

"Reb Yid," Chaim's face glowed, "you've got yourself a deal. And a guest for Shabbos."

The two Rosenstadters shook hands heartily and chuckled in anticipation.

That night, as they were walking home from shul together at a leisurely Shabbos pace, Yehudah started to ask Chaim about the new *shochet* who had come to town just before he'd left.

But Chaim urged him to wait until after they'd made kiddush. "After all," he reasoned, "the *balabusta* is probably waiting to serve us our meal, and if we get back much later than the others, we'll have to eat cold soup."

Yehudah wasn't so concerned about the temperature of the soup, but since Chaim was, he postponed his questions and hurried toward the boarding house together with his guest. "After all," he comforted himself, "there's the whole evening before us, and all day tomorrow."

Chaim wasted no time in starting *Shalom Aleichem* and *Eishes Chayil.* Then they made kiddush and washed.

Questions about people back home kept flitting through Yehudah's mind: "Don't forget to ask about Avraham the miller and Yosef the tailor. I wonder how the *rav's* youngest boy is — he'd been sick for some weeks when I left...."

But Yehudah held his tongue. It wouldn't take *that* long to eat a bowl of hot soup, so why create hard feelings and spoil a whole Shabbos, especially a special Shabbos like this one?

"Ahh..." gurgled Chaim with delight as his soup was served. Yehudah felt pangs of guilt as he saw with what relish Chaim devoured every last bit. "Ahh, that was something! Do you think..." Chaim leaned over towards Yehudah, "do

you think the *balabusta* would give me some
more? Especially those fluffy *kneidlach*? And
those *pupiks*...maybe she has an extra *pupik* left
in the pot?"

Yehudah was taken by surprise. Here he'd
struggled to be quiet and let Chaim enjoy his soup
undisturbed, even though he was just bursting
with questions. His own soup sat in front of him,
hardly touched, for he was too excited to eat. And
now — *another* bowl of soup?

But Yehudah silently argued with himself: "I
should stop another Jew from eating? And on
Shabbos? Here I have plenty, week after week;
when does poor Chaim ever get a chance to enjoy
such a *seudah*?"

Overcoming his impatience, Yehudah asked
the servant to refill Chaim's bowl. And he didn't
forget the *kneidlach* and the *pupiks*.

At last the second bowl of soup was finished.

"Now, Reb Chaim," Yehudah started off, beam-
ing, "tell me about home. How's Reb Avraham the
miller? How's his business doing? And is Avraham
himself well? How are his *kinderlach*? Is his Yossi
a *chasan* yet? Fine boy, that Yossi."

"Reb Avraham? Oh, he's fine," Chaim replied.
"They're all fine." Just then the servant went by
with a platter, and Chaim turned to look. "Ah,
farfel! And kugel! Just look at that kugel, Reb

Yehudah, and smell the aroma!" Chaim inhaled deeply as though a breeze from Gan Eden had just wafted in through the window. "Do they serve farfel and kugel here every week? And chicken! Look, he's bringing roast chicken, too...."

The menu was the least of Yehudah's concerns.

"Reb Avraham is well, you say?" he tapped Chaim on the hand to get his attention away from the neighboring table and back to his friend, the miller back home. "And how's business?"

"Fine, just fine, Reb Yehudah. Do they ever serve you *tzimmes* here?"

"And Yossi, is Reb Avraham's Yossi engaged yet?"

"Haven't heard anything. Do you think the kugel is made with noodles or potatoes?"

It was a losing battle. Yehudah knew he wasn't going to get the full report about Rosenstadt as long as the meal was being served. So he resigned himself to wait until after *birkas hamazon.*

Chaim outdid himself, thoroughly making up for his host's lack of appetite. Poor Yehudah just sat and watched, alternately amused, amazed, and annoyed. "At least *after* the meal he'll give me his full attention," he comforted himself silently.

After bentching, Yehudah rose from the table. "Come, Chaim, let's go into the sitting room, where we'll have some peace and quiet and you will be able to give me all the news without any interruptions."

Chaim wasn't as quick on his feet as Yehudah, but he dutifully plodded along behind him to a small room off to one side. There, he unceremoniously plopped himself down into the first armchair he found.

"That was some meal!" he commented to no one in particular. Then, looking directly at Yehudah, he asked, "What do they serve tomorrow? Will there be soup again? How's the cholent here? Do they have plenty of bones and a nice piece of beef for you?"

It was all Yehudah could do to refrain from screaming: "Bones?! Beef?! You just ate enough for a week!" But he held his tongue. After all, he reasoned, why ruin everything just when he was finally going to hear all the news? Instead, he ignored Chaim's queries about the next day's menu, and got down to business.

"Now, Chaim, tell me all about Reb David the *shochet*. Is he well? Is business all right? I mean, he still has enough of a *parnasah* even with that new young *shochet* who moved into town last year — what's his name, uh...Lazar — is he doing okay?"

Chaim looked as though two giant magnets were drawing his eyelids lower and lower. "Uh,

Lazar...*shochet*..." he mumbled. "Just fine," he managed to mumble before his head slumped forward and his lids closed completely. "Just fine," he whispered sleepily.

"No, not Lazar!" Yehudah jumped up and shook Chaim's shoulder. "David! I asked you about Reb David, not Lazar! Don't fall asleep on me now, Chaim. Wake up! Tell me the news. How's Reb David doing?"

"Fine. Just fine," Chaim pulled himself up with a start. "Everybody's just...cholent, and beans, and bones...."

"And his son, Chaim Mordechai?"

"Wonderful boy...uh, yes, Chaim...." The eyelids drooped again, and Chaim's chin fell right down onto his chest.

Reb Yehudah was desperate. Again he rose from his chair to shake Chaim out of his stupor. Just then, Chaim snored so loudly that he startled himself fully awake in a split second.

"Uh, yes...what was I saying? Uh, Lazar, Lazar — no, David; yes, beans, that is, uh...."

"Chaim Mordechai," Yehudah cut in impatiently. "You were telling me about Chaim Mordechai."

"Ah, yes, Chaim Morde...Mordechai..." his voice trailed off again as he sank into an even deeper sleep than before.

Thoroughly disgusted by now, Yehudah stalked out of the room and left for the *beis midrash.* Maybe learning the weekly *parashah* would help him forget how angry he was with Chaim.

What a disappointment! Now that he had started talking about all his friends back in Rosenstadt, he was more homesick than ever. "Well, maybe tomorrow," he consoled himself as he mounted the steps to the *beis midrash.* "Maybe tomorrow Chaim will have eaten all he wants and slept all he needs, and I'll get a chance to talk to him to my heart's content."

But the next day was no different. Kiddush, *hamotzi,* a steaming plate of cholent — and Chaim was already dozing off. It was all Yehudah could do to wake him up long enough to bentch.

"What's the idea?!" Yehudah fumed. "Here I give you a luxurious Shabbos, complete with a delicious meal such as you haven't had for years, a soft, warm bed, and on top of it all, three gold crowns. And all for what? *Not* so I could watch you gobble up one plate of cholent after another; *not* so I could see how you stuff yourself with roast chicken and farfel and kugel; *not* so I could listen to you snoring away. I gave you all this so you would spend time with *me,* so you would give me all your attention. That was our agreement, wasn't it?"

We know that on Shabbos, Hashem gives us an extra blessing, just as He gave *bnei Yisrael* an extra portion of manna for Shabbos in the desert. We have special clothes for Shabbos, special tablecloths, and a special goblet that we use only for kiddush. It's the same with our Shabbos candlesticks, and the special foods we eat. Some people eat in a different room on Shabbos, some people have special towels, special dishes, special shoes — each person tries to honor Shabbos in his own way. But all these special things are not the *purpose* of Shabbos. They're just the wrapping paper surrounding what should be the true content of Shabbos: a return to Hashem, to the closeness we experienced on that Shabbos long ago when the Torah was given to all of us at Har Sinai.

"Remember the day of Shabbos..." (Shemos 20:8). Of course, we all remember: cholent, treats, fancy clothing, shiny shoes. But is that what the Torah tells us to remember?

Let's look at the rest of the *pasuk*: "Remember the day of Shabbos *to keep it holy.*" The purpose of all the elegant clothes and special dishes is to set aside Shabbos as a day for Hashem, for His Torah and His mitzvos.

During the week, we have no choice but to devote our time and effort to making a living and taking care of the things our body needs. We all need homes to live in, clothes to wear, and food to eat. There is hardly time left to look after the needs of our *neshamos*, the part of us that can draw near to Hashem.

But on Shabbos, Hashem commands us to put aside all our worries about obtaining food to eat and clothes to wear. That way, we can use all our time and energy to spend Shabbos "with Hashem," so to speak.

If, instead, we fill our heads with weekday matters — like the latest fashions — or if our minds are only on Shabbos treats, then we're like sleepy Chaim, who didn't keep his agreement with Yehudah. Shabbos is for extra davening, learning, Tehillim, *chesed* — all the things that bring us closer to Hashem.

Vayikra

When is a House Not a House?

אָדָם כִּי יַקְרִיב מִכֶּם קָרְבָּן לַה' מִן הַבְּהֵמָה מִן הַבָּקָר וּמִן...
הַצֹּאן תַּקְרִיבוּ אֶת קָרְבַּנְכֶם.

*When anyone among you brings a korban to
Hashem, from beasts, cattle, and sheep you
shall bring your korban.*

(Vayikra 1:2)

This week we start reading the book of Vayikra. It contains many details about how to bring *korbanos* in the Holy Temple. When may we bring them? What should we bring? How much? Who may bring *korbanos* and who may not? There are many types of sacrifices, and several essential details to remember about each one.

But one point is essential regarding *all* the *korbanos*, as the Dubno Maggid makes clear in the following *mashal*:

Reb Shlomo and his wife were excited. They had finally decided to build a new house, and now they were sitting in the builder's office, waiting to sign the contract.

"Let's be sure to have a separate kitchenette for Pesach," said Mrs. Sofer, "and a big picture window in the kitchen so I can watch the children while they play in the yard."

"Whatever you like, dear," answered Reb Shlomo. "But all those are details. We'll have to remember to write them down later when the architect makes a blueprint for the new house. Right now, we're only signing the building contract."

Just then, Mr. Stone came in with the contract in his hand. He was followed by Mr. Glenn, the lawyer, and a secretary. Everything was ready. Both the Sofers and Mr. Stone read the contract and agreed that everything was in order. Smiling from ear to ear, Mr. Stone signed the contract and assured the Sofers that the house would be ready, just the way they wanted it, within a year's time.

Mrs. Sofer was a bit uneasy when she saw that the contract contained no details of how the house should be built, but Reb Shlomo assured her that all the details would be recorded afterwards in the blueprints.

"After all," he reasoned, "there's no sense going

into all the fine points of how high to make the ceilings, or what kind of roof to build, until Mr. Stone agrees in principle that he's willing to undertake the job of doing the construction for us."

Mrs. Sofer nodded in agreement, and together they headed for the office of the architect, Mr. Davis.

Now the Sofers — especially Mrs. Sofer — gave all the details of exactly how the living room should look, where the entrance hall should be, where the door to the dining room should be, how large the windows should be, and which way they should face.

Then they planned the dining room. Again they specified the size and shape of the room, how high the windows should be, where they needed electrical outlets, and where the doors should fit in.

So it went from one room to another. The Sofers described what they wanted, and the architect and his secretary wrote and wrote and wrote.

After they had finished planning the rooms, they began choosing building materials. Wood? What kind of wood? Metal? Steel? Aluminum? Concrete? And so it went — page after page of instructions and plans.

At last it was all done. The architect's secretary made an appointment for them to come back when the plans were all drawn up and the blue-prints ready for their signature.

It was a long three weeks for Mrs. Sofer, but at last they were on their way back to the architect's office to see the plans he had drawn up for their new home.

The Sofers were seated in the now familiar office, and the secretary came in carrying rolls and rolls of paper and a huge spiral notebook.

"Here are your plans!" explained the secretary cheerily. "Everything you asked for, and it's all here: floor plans, technical plans for electrical wiring, plumbing, plans for the heating and air-conditioning systems, and a full list of materials specifying exactly what quality and type of supplies will be used. Mr. Davis has everything down in black and white so there won't be any mistakes."

"I thought the contract we signed three weeks ago was long, but now I see it was nothing! Just look at this!" exclaimed Reb Shlomo, hefting the stack of papers to feel its full weight. "This is a whole book on its own!"

Just then, Mr. Davis came in. He briefly explained the various blueprints and lists and descriptions that made up the "book," and wished them good luck with the construction.

The Sofers thanked him warmly and took their

leave. They were anxious to get the plans back to Mr. Stone so the actual work of building their new home could start as soon as possible.

Mr. Stone received them pleasantly and leafed through the plans. "Looks fine," he said. "Mr. Davis has it all organized and listed. He does a very thorough job. Just leave this here with us, and our office will give you a call from time to time to let you know how things are going."

A few weeks passed before the Sofers received their first call: "We've got the cement and the light gray brick you wanted for the walls." Then two weeks later: "We have the special slate gray shingles for the roofing." Periodically, they received messages about the window frames, the plaster for the walls, and the wood paneling for the den. One week the secretary informed them that the bathroom fixtures had been delivered, and shortly afterwards the kitchen cupboards were due to arrive.

Things seemed to be moving at a good pace, and the Sofers spent hours discussing how to arrange the furniture in their new home, and how wonderful it would be to sit down to a meal in their new dining room and welcome guests into their spacious new living room. Each additional phone call fired their imagination to picture what life would be like in their new home; each time they grew more excited, and it became harder to wait for everything to be finished.

At last the call came: everything was ready!

The family could hardly wait. That same day they all piled into the car and drove to the site of their long-awaited new home. On the way, the children took turns asking questions about how the house would look from top to bottom. When Reb Shlomo told them that there was just one more corner to turn and then they'd finally see their new home, every nose was plastered to the car windows in anticipation of the glorious sight.

Slowly Rabbi Sofer turned the corner, and —

"Where is it? Here? That one over there?" the children all pounced on their father at once.

But Reb Shlomo wasn't even listening. His face was suddenly pale and stone-like. He stopped the car by the curb and just stared in disbelief.

"What is it, Shlomo? What happened?" Mrs. Sofer turned to her stricken husband. "Which is ours? Why are you so upset?"

Reb Shlomo turned off the motor and clambered out of the car, far too dumbstruck to say a word.

There on their lot stood not an inviting new home, but row after row of cinderblocks, window frames, bricks, and aluminum siding. There were stacks and stacks of roof shingles; rows of door frames leaning against each other like giant dominoes; heaps of pipes, taps and faucet handles; a display of sinks, cabinets, electrical wiring, and outlets; and light switches still in their original cartons and neatly labeled. Floor tiles and linoleum filled one corner of the lot. And in the "backyard," where they had hoped to find a lush, green lawn and a cool patio, their eyes met sack after dingy sack of gray, powdery cement leaning against piles of beams, planks, and plasterboard.

Mrs. Sofer was the first to speak:

"Are you sure this is the right place? Is this really *our* lot? What happened?"

"I don't know" was all Reb Shlomo could answer, shaking his head. "Let's go over to Mr. Stone's office."

Weaving their way through the stacks of wood and heaps of metal, they plodded back to the car. Even the children were silent as their father drove toward the office of Mr. Stone.

Once there, Reb Shlomo got straight to the point:

"We just went to see our new home," he began. "I don't understand, Mr. Stone. I don't understand at all. You agreed to have the house ready in a year. Your office phoned up to say that everything was seen to and that you'd finished the job. But you haven't even *begun*; you haven't hammered one nail into a plank or mixed one bag of cement with water. There isn't one wall up, much less a whole house. What did you mean by telling me the job was *finished*?"

Mr. Stone didn't say a word. Instead, he got up and went to a large, metal cupboard. It took him only a minute to find what he wanted: a duplicate of the blueprints and the technical description of the Sofers' new house.

He slapped the stack of plans and lists down on his desk and began to leaf through them.

"Here, look at this, Mr. Sofer. Here's a list of all the lumber required to build the house described in this blueprint. Now just go through this list and tell me what you think is missing." Mr. Stone thrust the list at the Sofers and waited, tense but silent, for their reply.

The Sofers couldn't find a thing missing; they started to explain that they weren't architects or contractors, so they didn't really understand all the details, but Mr. Stone had no time to listen to them.

He flipped through the large sheets of paper and found another list: Plumbing Fixtures and Accessories. "Anything missing here?" he demanded.

Then they went through the doors and windows, the electrical fixtures and wiring, and the heating/cooling system. Again and again, the

Sofers had to admit that they couldn't spot a single item on the lists that they hadn't seen in the stacks of building materials on their lot.

"So what's wrong? Why are you so upset? Here are the blueprints and the plans, and you yourself admit that there isn't one single screw or bolt missing!" exclaimed Mr. Stone, obviously bewildered. "I don't understand why you're unhappy with our work! We've done a perfect job, just like it says here in these one hundred forty-seven pages of instructions."

"But that's just the blueprint, Mr. Stone. You've forgotten all about the contract. Let's take out the contract and see what it says," declared Reb Shlomo, equally perturbed.

"The contract? Um...okay," said Mr. Stone, taken by surprise. "It was only a page or two as I recall, but we must have a copy of it on file. Miss Reit, could you please bring me a copy of the Sofers' contract?"

The secretary efficiently produced the two-page contract in record time. Both Mr. Stone and Reb Shlomo bent over the fine print to see what had been agreed upon.

"There!" pointed Reb Shlomo in relief. "You see? Your firm undertook to *build* the house for us, not just to purchase all the materials and assemble them on our lot. It says here 'to construct,' 'to erect said building' — and you haven't even begun the job. Getting everything together is only the first step, the preparation for the main project. All these months you've looked only at the blueprint, but you forgot that the blueprint was just an explanation of the *main* document, the contract. The main task is yet to be started!"

When Hashem told Moshe Rabbeinu that He was about to rescue the Jewish people from Egypt, He also told him what would happen afterward: "...when you take the people out of Egypt, you shall serve God on this mountain" (Shemos 3:12).

The "contract" stated that Hashem would take the Jews out of Egypt, and they would become His servants when they received the Torah at Har Sinai. Moshe Rabbeinu didn't know yet exactly *how* they would serve Hashem — the details would come later — but Hashem made it clear that this was the purpose of His taking the entire nation out of the land of Egypt.

As long as the Jews were slaves to Pharaoh, they were far too busy to worship Hashem. Thus, they had to leave Egypt. But that was only the beginning. The ultimate goal was to become servants of God.

That is what the Dubno Maggid wants to remind us of as we begin Vayikra: we must bring our sacrifices as servants of Hashem, in order to draw closer to Him, not just to go through the motions described in our "instruction book." This is the "contract" Hashem drew up with our forefathers before taking them out of Egypt: that they and their children, and their children's children after them, become servants of Hashem.

Nowadays our prayers must serve as our sacrifices: "...we will offer [the words of] our lips instead of oxen" (Hoshea 14:3). But the same principle holds true. If we only mumble the words with our lips instead of praying to Hashem with our hearts, we are assembling the raw materials while forgetting the main job: to use them to serve Hashem. Our contract is to use our prayers to shape our hearts and our very beings, to see the job through completely and become truly loyal servants of Hashem.

Erev Pesach

Remember the Main Point

וַיֹּאמֶר מֹשֶׁה אֶל הָעָם אַל תִּירָאוּ הִתְיַצְּבוּ וּרְאוּ אֶת יְשׁוּעַת
ה׳ אֲשֶׁר יַעֲשֶׂה לָכֶם הַיּוֹם כִּי אֲשֶׁר רְאִיתֶם אֶת מִצְרַיִם הַיּוֹם
לֹא תֹסִפוּ לִרְאֹתָם עוֹד עַד עוֹלָם.

Fear not! Stand ready and see the salvation of
Hashem, which He will perform for you this
day; for as you have seen Egypt today, you
shall never again see them unto all eternity.
(Shemos 14:13)

WHEN MOSHE RABBEINU led the Jewish nation out of Egypt, the people suddenly found themselves apparently trapped: ahead of them lay only the sea, and behind them Pharaoh's troops were advancing in hot pursuit. *Bnei Yisrael* were terrified that they would all be slaughtered there in the desert. They turned to Moshe Rabbeinu, trembling for their very lives, and he answered them: "Stand ready."

Why was it so important for the Jews to stand ready? Wouldn't Hashem's miracles have been just as impressive even if they had caught *bnei Yisrael* unaware?

The Dubno Maggid addresses this point in the following *mashal*:

The duke of Frischburg was a well-known figure for miles around. His spacious castle towered high on the hill overlooking Frischburg. His elegant carriage and majestic white steeds were recognized by all. Those who had been privileged to see the interior of the castle spoke of unimaginable treasures stored within: paintings, chandeliers, carpets, and tapestries all adorned long corridors and high-ceilinged rooms that defied description. And when meals were served, visitors forgot to eat; they were too busy gaping at the magnificent serving dishes to pay attention to the food within. No one was sure exactly how many silver platters, golden candlesticks, and crystal decanters and serving bowls the duke's cupboards and storehouse contained, but one thing was agreed upon by all: it would be an unforgettable experience to have a peek at the duke's vast riches.

Some people spoke of a wondrous, forty-eight-branch candelabrum with dozens of exquisite silver roses to hold the burning tapers. Two proudly roaring golden lions reared up high on their hind legs and grasped the main stem of the candelabrum with their front paws. Even more amazing, underneath the lions there was said to be a key that could turn the lamp into a music box, which played the duke's favorite tune in crisp, sweet tones that sounded like mystical silver bells.

Then there was the bird cage. What rumors circulated about the golden bird cage! Its graceful wire frame shone, they said, like the setting sun at the end of a perfect summer's day. "Soft, shiny gold," people whispered in awe. And as if the magic glow of the cage were not enough, here, too, there was a secret key. When it was wound up, the golden cage came alive with song and movement as the colorful stuffed bird inside bobbed up and down in time to the delicate notes produced by the hidden music box. They said that the duke took out the golden cage only once a year, on his birthday, to delight his daughter, Amalia, who waited anxiously from year to year to catch a glimpse of it once again.

Other treasures included rare gems, a sapphire diadem, a magnificent ebony chess set inlaid with ivory and precious stones, and a huge, hand-crafted globe that actually rotated on its axis every twenty-four hours when wound up and set in motion.

However, the duke was wont to say that his most precious treasure was not his gold, his silver, or his rare jewels. It was his beloved daughter Amalia, whom he cherished above all.

Years passed, and Amalia grew into a young woman. Naturally, when the time came for the duke to find her a husband, none but the finest, noblest, and most learned of scholars would do. Messengers were sent to comb the kingdom looking for the most promising young scholar. High and low the duke's men searched, and returned with several fine candidates. The excitement grew. Who would be chosen to become Amalia's husband and the next duke of Frischburg?

Some favored one young contender, others another, but no one could overlook the tall, noble Collin, whose gracious bearing and refinement set him apart from all his competitors. Something else about Collin also set tongues wagging, though no one dared mention it aloud or even whisper it in the presence of the duke. Rumor had it that Collin's father was a nobleman who had died when his son was only a baby, leaving his family penniless. The noble Collin had grown up knowing hunger and cold and misery; it was only his aristocratic birth and exceptional talents that had secured him a chance to study together with the sons of the richest nobles in the land. Once accepted to the highest universities, Collin's exceptional mind and patrician air had placed him head and shoulders above all the others. But poor he remained; as yet, he had not started to practice any profession, and when the duke's messengers selected him to appear in Frischburg, he had to borrow clothing and funds just to make the trip.

The duke was aware of Collin's predicament, but it only served to increase his admiration for this unique prodigy. "He lacks only wealth; he has all the other qualities I seek — much more so than the other candidates," the duke decided after interviewing them all. "Wealth is no problem: I need only grant him a portion of my own resources and assign him some of my lands. Then Collin will be the most suitable choice by far!" The duke's mind was made up: "Collin shall wed Amalia and become my heir!"

The tongues that had whispered stealthily now jabbered endlessly.

"A pauper, the duke's heir!"

"Imagine, Lady Amalia wed to the impoverished Collin!"

But the duke soon changed all that. He outfitted Collin royally, and presented him with lavish engagement presents. Plans were made for the wedding, which promised to be the most extravagant celebration Frischburg had ever known.

Now tongues started wagging about the duke's fabulous treasures. The famous silver platters, crystal goblets, and gilded china bowls would all come out of the cupboards and be on view when the wedding banquet was served. And who could tell? Maybe the duke would display some of his other treasures. Speculation ran high in Frischburg. Perhaps, at long last, *everyone* would get to see even the golden bird cage, and the candelabrum of silver roses, and the sapphire diadem and...and...there was no end to the conjecturing about which unimaginable wonders would grace the tables and entertain the guests when the wedding day finally arrived.

Only the groom himself was not caught up in the excitement. Newly garbed in a luxurious wardrobe fit for the duke of Frischburg, Collin had returned to his studies for a final few weeks. Now he was elegantly dressed and much celebrated amongst his fellow students. Even though he knew he would soon become a wealthy noble, Collin still had only the most meager of meals to keep body and soul together, and he lived on excitement and concentrated study as much as on simple bread and water.

At last it was time to return to Frischburg for the wedding. Just as the townsfolk had predicted, the duke emptied his treasure chest in honor of his beloved Amalia and her future husband. Nothing was left on the shelves. Silver glittered, gold shone; diamonds, rubies, and sapphires sparkled. Platter after platter of roast duckling, pheasant, and venison went untouched as everyone had eyes only for the fabled wonders the duke had his staff display. No one asked for second helpings; silver goblets full of vintage wines remained almost ignored as the assemblage of guests gave their full attention to the captivating golden cage and the bobbing bird within, and the crowns, chalices, and bejeweled trinkets that extended from one end of the banquet hall to the other.

Only one person seemed to be concerned with all the tempting dishes that the kitchen staff had labored to prepare. That person was none other than the bridegroom himself. Accustomed to staving off his hunger with plain bread and an occasional boiled potato, Collin was completely dazzled by the vast selection of new foods before him, and totally preoccupied with tasting the myriad royal delicacies that adorned the table. So overwhelmed was he at the array of food that he barely noticed the exhibits around him. Even the magical bird cage and its dainty music failed to register in his mind as he bit into a luscious, ripe strawberry and a juicy mandarin, fruits he had heard of and seen but never tasted.

The evening of festivities came to an end, and the well-wishers took their leave of the duke and the young couple and went their separate ways. But it was weeks and weeks before talk of the duke's fabulous riches died down.

Collin, now a resident of Frischburg, also heard the vivid descriptions of the wonders his father-in-law's treasuries housed, and gradually he began to ponder: "Why don't I remember the silver roses on that stupendous candelabrum? And the sapphire diadem? And the bird cage! How wonderful to see such a sight! Where was I when the bird cage was displayed?"

The more he heard the stable boys and kitchen hands discussing what they had seen at his very own wedding, the more curious Collin became. He, too, had to behold all these delights. He decided to approach his father-in-law with his request that very day.

"My lord," Collin bowed to the duke. "I would like to ask another favor, in addition to all the kindnesses you have already so graciously bestowed on me."

"What is it, Collin?"

"My lord is reputed to have an incomparable collection of marvelous treasures. I, too, would like to see the vast array of rare, precious gems, and the silver and gold vessels, and the fabulous bird cage that I have heard so much about."

"What? You, of all people, should ask to see my collection of gems and treasures? You, Collin? Why, it was only in *your* honor that I put everything on display at once, for the very first time in my life. Why didn't you look at everything then, when I showed it to you? If you were too busy eating to take advantage of the unique opportunity I gave you, you missed your chance. You should have used your time better at the wedding. Now it's too late."

At Yam Suf, Moshe Rabbeinu first told the Jews not to be afraid. Then he commanded them to stand ready and see the wonders and miracles Hashem would perform to save them. Finally, he warned them that only this one time would they see such awe-inspiring *nissim* and mighty acts of Hashem; therefore, they must be careful to pay attention fully, and not be afraid.

Fear can confuse a person so much that he becomes blind to what is before his very eyes. That is why Moshe Rabbeinu first commanded the people not to be afraid, and then told them to "stand ready" and witness the wonders Hashem was about to show them. This was their unique opportunity to see the power of Hashem revealed so openly that no one could ever say, "It was only a coincidence," or "It was only natural." The *pasuk* tells us that this time even the Egyptians admitted: "*God* is fighting for them" (Shemos 14:25). This was no commonplace event to be explained by the "laws of nature" or military strategy. It was the obvious intervention of a Supreme Power Who could control the laws of science and nature as He wished. There was no other explanation for what happened.

Even as the waters of Yam Suf shifted to the right and left, letting *Am Yisrael* pass through safely, the towering walls of water flanking the Egyptian forces suddenly crashed down upon them thunderously. In a flash, Hashem had transformed them back into ordinary sea water when Moshe Rabbeinu stretched forth his hand over Yam Suf as he had been commanded. It was then that *Am Yisrael* "saw the great hand that Hashem had wielded in Egypt, and the people feared God and trusted in God and in Moshe, His servant" (14:31).

Each year, we, too, have an opportunity that it doesn't pay to miss. Rav Eliyahu Dessler, *zt"l,* explains that each Yom Tov gives us the chance to relive what *klal Yisrael* experienced thousands of years ago. On Shavuos, we have a chance to feel the way *Am Yisrael* did at Har Sinai when the Torah was given to us by Hashem Himself. On

Sukkos, we can feel Hashem's protection enveloping us, as *bnei Yisrael* did in the wilderness. And on Pesach, we have a golden opportunity to feel the hand of Hashem rescuing us from Egyptian slavery and fighting our enemies with open miracles — if only we open our eyes to see them.

The night of the seder is devoted to recounting the details of these miracles. But we must "stand ready," for many things can blind us. The beautiful dishes on the seder table, our shiny new shoes, heated debates over *afikoman* prizes — all these can make us miss out on the indescribable miracles we have a chance to re-experience on seder night, even though these miracles were performed for *our* benefit, and ours alone, and we should be the first to be aware of them.

This Pesach, remember to "stand ready"; enjoy your new Yom Tov outfit, and the special treats and excitement, but don't become a "Collin" who says afterwards: "Where was I?"

Remember, the main point of Pesach is to tell and retell — and relive — the wonders and *nissim* Hashem performed for us in *yetzias Mitzrayim*, so that we, too, will "see the great hand Hashem wielded" against the Egyptians, and we, too, will fear Hashem and trust in Him alone.

Shemini

Hashem, the Master Healer

וַיַּקְרִיבוּ לִפְנֵי ה׳ אֵשׁ זָרָה אֲשֶׁר לֹא צִוָּה אוֹתָם. וַתֵּצֵא אֵשׁ
מִלִּפְנֵי ה׳ וַתֹּאכַל אוֹתָם וַיָּמֻתוּ לִפְנֵי ה׳.

*And Nadav and Avihu, the sons of Aharon...of-
fered strange fire before Hashem, which He'd
commanded them not. And a fire went forth
from Hashem and devoured them, and they
died before Hashem.*

(Vayikra 10:1-2)

What can we learn from this strange epi-
sode in the Torah? The Dubno Maggid
offers a *mashal*:

It was Lord Stonehill's big day. After three years
of planning, organizing, and building, the

model city of Greenville was ready to receive its first residents. Lord Stonehill had selected upright citizens of good standing from the long list of applicants. Careful consideration had been given to choosing a balanced selection of merchants and craftsmen. After all, it wouldn't do to have an abundance of carpenters and wheelwrights but no blacksmiths in a model town like Greenville.

A short walk around the new city quickly let the visitor see for himself that this was not just another dot on the map. Greenville boasted wide, airy avenues lined with graceful elm trees and lordly oaks, which stretched straight as an arrow from one side of the town to the other. Every few blocks, one came upon a delightful park with lush, well-tended lawns and gaily colored flower beds. Lord Stonehill had even ordered Greenville's gardeners to plant a variety of fruit trees with fragrant blossoms. This way, the town would be blessed year-round with luscious apples, cherries, oranges, and mandarins, and the air would be scented with budding fruits. Large ponds, quaint bridges, and twisting pathways through leafy woods all combined to make Greenville the most perfect hometown one could ever hope for.

Lord Stonehill had spared neither effort nor expense and today he surveyed the fruit of his efforts with deep satisfaction.

To be sure he had overlooked nothing, Lord Stonehill decided to call in an expert to give him an outsider's opinion. So he summoned the famous Professor Sharf and asked him to evaluate the new town and its needs.

The professor spent several days touring Greenville, interviewing the residents, and taking notes. Then he made an appointment with Lord Stonehill to discuss his findings.

"On the whole, it is a wonderful place!" Professor Sharf reported to him. "Well-planned, solidly built — a first-class piece of work. In fact, there is only one thing I found missing. Correct me if I'm wrong, my lord, but I think there isn't a single doctor to be found in all of Greenville."

"Ah, a doctor! Of course! How could I have forgotten about that? Thank you, Professor. You're so right. One cannot and must not leave an entire town with no medical care. Especially a model town like Greenville. Thank you ever so much for your fine advice. I shall see to it at once!"

That same day, messages went out to all the leading hospitals and universities, asking for help in finding the most expert physician in the country.

"Whatever salary is requested, we will pay it," wrote Lord Stonehill, "so long as we have the foremost medical authority there is."

Replies soon came pouring in and Lord Stonehill selected the man he wanted: Dr. Geftman. Further letters were exchanged and a date was set for Dr. Geftman's move to Greenville.

Word of the famous doctor's impending arrival quickly spread. On the appointed day, the townspeople gathered in the city's largest square to welcome their new physician royally. Even the nobles from surrounding areas came to join in the festivities.

"Welcome to Greenville, the model city!" boomed Lord Stonehill, leading Dr. Geftman into the town hall for the official reception. Nobles and dignitaries followed the two men into the spacious hall, where greetings were exchanged and a lively discussion soon developed.

"Let's find someone sick so the good doctor can display his talents to us right away," suggested one of the young aristocrats. "Anyone know somebody who's ill?"

One young fellow stepped forward and said, "I do. Truth to tell, I have a nagging headache that I'd like to get rid of."

Dr. Geftman asked Lord Stonehill to have the patient and himself taken to the offices that had been prepared and equipped for him. There he examined the fellow and gave him medications.

"I want you to remain here a few days so I can

look after you properly," the doctor explained.

The patient agreed, and the whole town set to talking about what a devoted and skilled physician it had gained:

"Isn't Harold lucky! Imagine being chosen to be Dr. Geftman's first patient in Greenville. You can be sure he'll get the best treatment possible. Surely Dr. Geftman is anxious to prove himself to us, and will spare no effort and no expense to cure him."

Indeed, Dr. Geftman prescribed rare and expensive drugs for Harold, but he didn't get better. The doctor ordered new treatments and different medications, and hovered over his patient day and night. But eventually, to everyone's disbelief, poor Harold died.

Now tongues were wagging furiously. What had happened? How could it be? Their famous Dr. Geftman, the man who was renowned for tackling the most hopeless of cases, had not only failed to cure a simple headache in an apparently healthy young noble, but he had even let him die. Greenville was horror-struck!

Lord Stonehill was at a total loss. Dr. Geftman had been recommended to him as the greatest expert of their times — "nearly a reviver of the dead," one professor had written. What had gone wrong? Lord Stonehill summoned the doctor and demanded an explanation.

"He was only suffering from a common headache. He didn't even look ill," Lord Stonehill reminded the doctor. "If someone hadn't gone looking for a potential patient, we would never even have known he wasn't feeling well.

"If your examination showed that he was incurable, why did you invest so much time and effort in his case? Why did you prescribe such expensive, rare drugs? Now you've ruined your reputation among the people and they won't have faith in you anymore. Why did you do it?"

"My esteemed Lord Stonehill," Dr. Geftman bowed low, "please do not be so distressed. Let me explain.

"Although Harold appeared to be quite hale and hearty, he was in fact suffering from a serious, internal illness. I thought there was a chance that I might cure him, but I am only a human being, not a miracle worker. Unfortunately, I was not able to save him.

"But there is one aspect of Harold's death that consoles me, and I believe that it will comfort you, who wish only Greenville's benefit, as well. It is this:

"Ever since my arrival in Greenville, the townspeople have decided that they no longer need to live sensibly and be reasonably careful about their health. They feel they can eat whatever they like, as much as they like, and whenever they like. It doesn't matter if they make themselves sick because they have the famous Dr. Geftman here to cure them. If they stay out in the rain, or don't sleep enough, or strain themselves dancing and drinking at silly parties until the middle of the night, there's nothing to worry about. Dr. Geftman will cure their headaches and ease their hoarse throats and bleary, red eyes. Young men race about on horses but they have no fear — Dr. Geftman will heal their broken bones! Then they drink themselves right up to death's door without a second thought or a moment's worry. 'Dr. Geftman can revive the dead,' they tell themselves. 'Certainly he'll be able to revive me.'

"So you see, my lord, instead of being a blessing for Greenville, instead of promoting *better* health for all, as you so sincerely wished, my coming here has endangered everyone's health. I cannot revive the dead, nor can I heal those who choose to live recklessly and then rely on me to cure them miraculously. In the end they will all die and then claim that I am a poor doctor, or no doctor at all.

"Now that poor Harold has died, the others can clearly see that I do not work miracles, and I cannot cure those who don't take care of themselves. Let each one know that he himself is responsible for his well-being and must eat and sleep and live according to the rules of good health. After what happened to Harold, I hope the whole town has learned its lesson and will take the proper health precautions from now on."

At the time of *matan Torah*, all of *Am Yisrael* became completely healthy in mind, heart, and body. The entire Jewish nation promised with all its heart to keep every detail of Hashem's commandments.

But Hashem knew that the germs of the *yetzer hara* would eventually attack our hearts and minds, and we would sometimes do *aveiros*.

At that time, we would be "ill"; we would need treatment that would make our hearts healthy and faithful to Hashem again.

Therefore, Hashem told us to build the *mishkan* and bring sacrifices there. He taught us exactly which *korban* would cure each kind of spiritual disease, and provided full details about how to prepare the "medications" — the *korbanos* — and how to administer them.

On the first day of Nissan, the *mishkan* was completed. *Klal Yisrael* spent seven days dedicating it according to Hashem's instructions.

On the eighth day, *klal Yisrael* was about to start using the *mishkan* to serve Hashem. What a

joyous day for the Jewish nation! Imagine having
— right in the middle of town — a famous medical
center where any illness or injury can be cured!

Similarly, *bnei Yisrael* knew that, from now on,
whenever they became "infected" by the germs of
the *yetzer hara*, there was a guaranteed cure all
ready and waiting: the *mishkan* and its *korbanos*.

But Hashem knew that there was also a danger in the *mishkan*. People might think that now
they needn't be afraid of the *yetzer hara*, that
doing an *aveirah* was no longer a tragic loss. They
might say, "We can always set things right by
running to the *mishkan* and bringing the *korban*
Hashem prescribed for this *aveirah*. Then we'll be
healthy again."

Such an attitude would turn the *mishkan* into
a reason *not* to be careful about mitzvos. Instead
of helping people come closer to Hashem, the
korbanos would, *chas vechalilah*, do the opposite.

Just as we were about to start using the
mishkan to serve Hashem, something happened
to prevent this mistake: Two of the greatest
tzaddikim alive, sons of Aharon, the *kohen gadol*,
tried to bring a sacrifice that Hashem had not
asked for, and they were killed by a Heavenly fire
right in the *mishkan* itself!

Now there could be no mistake. All of *klal
Yisrael* saw that even the holy *mishkan*, even the

korbanos themselves, could never become a substitute for unbending obedience to Hashem. Now the *mishkan* could serve its true purpose: to bring *klal Yisrael* closer to Hashem and His Torah and mitzvos.

Tazria

Choosing Sides

זֹאת תּוֹרַת הַבְּהֵמָה וְהָעוֹף וְכֹל נֶפֶשׁ הַחַיָּה הָרֹמֶשֶׂת בַּמַּיִם
וּלְכָל נֶפֶשׁ הַשֹּׁרֶצֶת עַל הָאָרֶץ. לְהַבְדִּיל בֵּין הַטָּמֵא וּבֵין
הַטָּהֹר.... אִשָּׁה כִּי תַזְרִיעַ וְיָלְדָה זָכָר וְטָמְאָה שִׁבְעַת
יָמִים....

*This is the law of the beasts, the birds, every
living creature that moves in the water, and
every creature that creeps on the earth. To
distinguish between the impure and the
pure.... When a woman conceives and gives
birth to a male, she shall be impure seven
days...*

(Vayikra 11:46-47; 12:2)

I N LAST WEEK'S *parashah, Shemini,* the Torah
started teaching us the laws of *taharah* (purity)
and *tumah* (impurity), specifying which animals, insects, fish, and birds are *tahor* and which
are not.

The beginning of *parashas Tazria* carries on with *tumah* and *taharah*, explaining how people become *tamei* and how they make themselves *tahor* again.

At first glance, it seems strange that the Torah discusses people after animals, birds, and even grasshoppers. But the Torah has a special reason for this order, as the Dubno Maggid explains in the following *mashal*:

Dokan had a problem. Born and raised in Hopistan, he had always been a loyal patriot of his native land. But now he had a tempting offer: to become a well-paid soldier in the army of a neighboring country, Keeland. His present job as an assistant carpenter was sometimes boring, and he was jealous of the generous praise and honor heaped upon his boss, the master carpenter. Then there were the high prices his products commanded while he, Dokan, sanded and sawed and polished his heart away day after day, earning what seemed like mere pennies in comparison.

Now, Dokan mused to himself, all that might change. Army life would be exciting. He would see new places, wear a snappy uniform, and — when he rose in rank — become a respected personality, ordering the young privates to do whatever he liked, even polish his boots.

The more Dokan daydreamed about it, the more glamorous the idea became. Only the pleadings of his friend Matoon held him back.

"Think of all the dangers! Why sell yourself to the army? Remember, once you sign up, you have no choice but to follow orders, go where they send you, and do whatever your commander says. Why, there might even be a war between Hopistan and Keeland! Then what would you do?

"Better stick it out another few years in the wood shop until you become a master carpenter. Finish your training and make yourself a name as a master craftsman. Once you establish your reputation, you'll have a respectable income for life, without risking your life running off to war."

But it was too late. Captivated by dreams of adventure, shiny medals of honor, and rich booty taken in battle, Dokan crossed the border to Keeland and enlisted in the local army for five years.

The time passed quickly and Dokan enjoyed himself thoroughly. He marched, he drilled, and he learned to fight, run, and spy. Each day brought new thrills and challenges. Forgotten were the dull days of hammer and saw, forgotten was his native Hopistan; even his good friend Matoon remained only a distant if fond memory. Dokan was delighted with his decision to enlist and merely smiled knowingly to himself when he recalled how Matoon had naively urged him to bide his time patiently in the carpentry shop.

Then it happened: war broke out between Keeland and Hopistan. The armies encamped a few miles from each other and prepared for battle.

One night Dokan was summoned to the commandant's tent. Several others were present, and Dokan noted with pride that the group included some of the most respected young officers in the battalion. His chest puffed out another inch or two as he listened to the group's assignment.

"Tonight you will reconnoiter the enemy's camp," the commander began. "Each one of you has been handpicked for the job."

It was a dangerous mission, to be sure, but Dokan was beyond fear. Surely success would mean promotion, another medal, fame. His head was spinning just at the thought of it all.

It was hard to wait for night to fall, but at last it was dark. Dokan joined the others, tense with excitement. His fame, his future, and his fortune all depended on victory!

At first everything went smoothly. They crossed the valley silently, avoided the first sentry they met, and started up the hill. Then, just as they mounted the crest, the very worst happened: ambush! A scouting party of Hopistanis had them surrounded.

In seconds the squad of elite commanders

dissolved into a handful of helpless prisoners of war, bound, gagged, and broken in spirit. Only one of them, Dokan, took action. Motioning and grunting repeatedly, he made the guards understand that he had something important to tell them. They loosened his gag and let him speak.

"You're making a mistake!" Dokan yelled excitedly. "I'm not from Keeland; I'm a native Hopistani, just like you fellows. I only joined up with them," he nodded in the direction of his captive comrades, "to make my fortune fast. But I'm really a Hopistani at heart. I don't belong with them. I just *look* like them for now, but really I'm one of you. Set me free! It's a mistake!"

"You fool!" thundered the guards in fury. "You're the one who made the mistake. You're no Hopistani. You forfeited that title years ago when you signed up with the Keelanders and started taking orders from them. Why, if we hadn't caught you in time, you might be putting your knife in the back of a Hopistani sentry right this very minute. You're no different from any of the others. You sold yourself to them, and now you'll share their fate. Tie him up! Take him away!"

A human being can, and should, be absolutely distinct from animals. Only humans are created *betzelem Elokim,* in the image of God. It is this Divine spark that distinguishes man from beast. True, people have certain animal instincts, like eating, drinking, and resting. But we Jews eat and sleep only in order to have the energy to do mitzvos and learn Torah. We eat and sleep according to the instructions Hashem has given us, because it is His will that we be healthy.

Animals can't help but follow their bodily instincts. They eat because they're hungry, sleep because they're tired, and fight or run away because they're afraid. They have no awareness of Hashem's rewards or punishments because these aren't meant for them. They have no need for language — the special tool of man alone — so they were not created with the power of speech.

In contrast, human beings can either follow their instincts or follow Hashem's instructions. The *yetzer hara* encourages us to listen to our body's desires; Hashem rewards us when, instead, we listen to His commandments.

The choice is ours and, like Dokan, we must accept the consequences. Which army are we going to join? Whom are we going to serve, Hashem or, *lehavdil,* the *yetzer hara?* Who is our commanding officer, and which "uniform" are we going to wear?

The choice is ours and ours alone.

Acharei Mos
My Son, My Firstborn

וְלֹא תָקִיא הָאָרֶץ אֶתְכֶם בְּטַמַּאֲכֶם אֹתָהּ כַּאֲשֶׁר קָאָה אֶת הַגּוֹי
אֲשֶׁר לִפְנֵיכֶם. כִּי כָּל אֲשֶׁר יַעֲשֶׂה מִכֹּל הַתּוֹעֵבֹת הָאֵלֶּה
וְנִכְרְתוּ הַנְּפָשׁוֹת הָעֹשֹׂת מִקֶּרֶב עַמָּם.

*But [you shall not cause] the land to spew you
out when you defile it, as it spewed out the
nations that were before you. For whoever
commits any of these abominations, those
souls who perform them will be cut off from the
midst of their people.*

(Vayikra 18:28-29)

THE END OF *parashas Acharei Mos* lists
several *aveiros* that were common among
the Canaanites who lived in Eretz Yisrael
before *Am Yisrael* conquered it under Yehoshua.

Hashem then cautions us that if, Heaven forbid, the Jews persist in the same sins as the

Canaanites, they too will be driven from Eretz Yisrael, but in a far worse way.

Why must the Jews be threatened with both *kareis* and expulsion from Eretz Yisrael? Isn't it enough of a punishment to be driven from our land?

The Dubno Maggid explains with a *mashal*:

Lord Glenn was determined to prepare his beloved only son, Ernest, for a brilliant career as an aristocrat and parliamentary leader. Only the finest tutors would do for the young Ernest. And to make his studies more enjoyable and give the boy some competition, Lord Glenn found a talented orphan lad the same age to serve as his companion.

Ernest and Ronald studied together, ate together, and shared a bedroom, and when the day's lessons were completed, they romped the grassy hills and dales of Lord Glenn's vast estate as though they were twins.

Only as they grew somewhat older did the differences between the two become apparent.

Ernest remained a studious, diligent pupil, while Ronald tended to daydream and fall behind. Occasionally, he even failed to appear in the special corner of the library set aside for their lessons. When accosted by his geometry or French tutor, Ronald would mumble something about a headache, but Ernest knew that his erstwhile companion felt well enough to hunt down several rabbits in the grassy woods beyond the stables. Ronald was simply not a scholar. Latin, French, and mathematics were not for him. But he feared Lord Glenn's wrath so he escaped to the open fields, where he became an expert at mischief and at making excuses.

Of course, it was not long before Lord Glenn discovered the truth: Ronald was dishonest; he was taking advantage of the luxuries of the castle to loaf and get into trouble.

The very next morning, Lord Glenn sent him away with a stern warning not to come back.

Ernest continued his studies alone. But as the weeks passed, spring approached and he, too, became restless. Latin verbs and Greek history no longer interested him. From his treks in the woods with Ronald, he knew that the creek must be gurgling away while frogs kerplunked into the sparkling water and squirrels and rabbits darted along the newly green branches. Right this very moment, Ronald was probably lolling along some creek or river bank tossing pebbles, while here he was trapped indoors, glued to a hard, oaken chair and doomed to reckoning the areas of triangles.

Next morning, Ernest's mind was made up.

Ronald had played hookey many a time before he was caught. He, Ernest, would do it just once — he would run wild in the woods the whole glorious morning. Just one day's freedom, he told himself, and then he would be able to concentrate again the way he used to in the old days, with Ronald.

That morning, he told his history teacher that his head ached, and left "to go lie down until his mind cleared." It didn't take him more than five minutes to let himself out the scullery door and head for the stables. From there he was up the hill and onto the banks of the creek before anyone noticed he had left. He reveled in every chirp and croak, every fresh, green bud and blossom, until the evening shadows warned him to hasten home.

"Ernest!" thundered Lord Glenn upon his arrival. "Ernest!"

"Yes, my lord," Ernest barely managed to reply.

"Come into my study, Ernest. At once!"

The boy's legs reluctantly carried him into the study. Lord Glenn rarely lost his temper, but Ernest knew that when he did....

Five minutes later Ernest stood alone in the study, muffling his sobs, far too sore to sit down. It was the first time since he had left the nursery that his father had hit him. Lord Glenn had been furious beyond words, and Ernest was thoroughly bewildered. Had he done *such* a terrible thing? Was he any worse than Ronald? It had taken weeks until Ronald was caught, and even then, all his father had done was send him away with a scolding. In fact, Ronald hadn't been slapped even once during his years as Ernest's companion. Why, then, should Ernest, whom Lord Glenn certainly loved more than Ronald, suffer so?

But Ernest knew better than to argue with his father at the height of his fury. He had taken his punishment without saying a word.

Several hours later, Lord Glenn's mood had obviously improved. Ernest caught him humming a tune as he relaxed after winning a close game of chess with his good friend and frequent rival across the board, Lord Winter. Now, Ernest thought, would be a good time to approach his father with his question.

"My lord, may I ask something?"

"What would you care to know, Ernest?"

"I am perplexed. My former companion, Ronald, surely owed you a great debt. You fed and clothed him, educated him, and showed him great kindness. When he disobeyed you, when he betrayed your trust, all you did was stop doing him favors. That is, you sent him away. But you didn't strike him or cause him any pain. You didn't ask him to repay your expenses, nor did you impose any kind of punishment on him. You just stopped helping him.

"I'm your only son. Surely you love me no less than Ronald. Why did you give *me* such a severe punishment? Why, indeed, did it make you so angry the very first morning that I misbehaved?"

"Ernest, my boy, what is there to compare? Who is that Ronald to me? I am not his father, or even his uncle or cousin. I have no ties with him. So long as I thought he was helping you achieve the goals I have set for you, I kept him here in the castle and treated him decently. But when it became clear that he was a bad influence, I no longer wanted him in my home. I sent him away, and I'm no longer concerned with him. He is not my son, after all. It's not my responsibility to make him behave.

"But when *you* misbehave, what shall I do? How can I send you away? You're my own flesh and blood, my only son. I am responsible for you. And for you, I have great hopes and desires: to see you grow, develop your talents, and perfect your character.

"I can't just forget about you; I have to punish you so you will stop misbehaving and do as you are told. And I won't leave you until I see that you are really achieving all the goals I have set for you, even if I have to punish you again and again."

A Jew who sins, *chas vechalilah*, is punished more severely, because we are Hashem's own children. As Hashem says of us, "Israel is My son, My firstborn" (Shemos 4:22). Hashem will never just send us away and "forget" about us, for we are His own, His dear ones, as the *parashah* concludes: "*Ani Hashem Elokeichem* — I am Hashem, *your* God" (Vayikra 18:30).

Hashem is telling us: "I am your Father, Who loves you, and I shall never abandon you to your sins and your evil impulse, even if I must punish you time and again, for I am Hashem, *your* God, Who loves you and looks after you."

Emor

Have I Changed So Much?

וּבְקֻצְרְכֶם אֶת קְצִיר אַרְצְכֶם לֹא תְכַלֶּה פְּאַת שָׂדְךָ בְּקֻצְרֶךָ
וְלֶקֶט קְצִירְךָ לֹא תְלַקֵּט לֶעָנִי וְלַגֵּר תַּעֲזֹב אֹתָם אֲנִי ה'
אֱלֹקֵיכֶם.

*And when you reap the harvest of your land,
you shall not remove the corner [peah] of your
field when you reap, nor shall you gather any
gleaning [leket] of your harvest — you shall
leave them to the poor and the stranger; I am
Hashem, your God.*

(Vayikra 23:22)

W hy does Hashem "reintroduce" Himself
after commanding the Jewish people to
be charitable?

According to Rashi, He is reminding us that
He will surely reward us for observing this mitzvah. But isn't that true of all mitzvos? Why are

peah and *leket* singled out?

The Dubno Maggid explains with a *mashal*:

Shimon had never been famous for his good luck, but now he seemed to have hit rock bottom. "It just can't get worse," he thought. His empty purse hardly made a bulge in his pocket as he pressed a hand against his thighbone. "That fall outside the last town I visited has left me half-crippled," he muttered to himself. The rheumatism that used to come and go now seemed to be here for good. All his bones and joints ached, reminding him again and again that he wasn't getting any younger. Peddling housewares was a youngster's job. Many a time he had promised himself that he would look for something easier, something that wouldn't aggravate the pain in his joints, but nothing seemed to turn up.

But now he had no choice as he reached the crossroads and turned right onto the road leading to Zelstadt. He would be forced to lay down his peddler's pack once and for all.

His eyes fell on the signpost.

Ah, Zelstadt! Just to think of his hometown made his heart lighter. Here people knew him and always welcomed him warmly. The rebbetzin would surely invite him in for a hearty meal, and when she heard of his hard luck — how he had lost many of his customers to younger, sharper traders, fellows who could afford a horse and cart and offered a wider variety of pots and pans and ribbons and cloths for the village women to choose from — surely she would speak to the rabbi about finding him some other kind of work, something more suited to his age and his aching bones.

Shimon came to another crossroads, lowered his pack, and sat down to rest. A glance at the sun told him that he would be hard-pressed to reach Zelstadt before the sun set. His eyes wandered along the path that led to the Jewish inn behind a grove of pines across the road. A pair of travelers made their way up the path towards the inn. Shimon couldn't help being jealous. In better times, he too had gone his merry way along that path, knowing full well that a warm welcome and a hot bowl of soup awaited him within. How he would enjoy a plate of steaming broth this very minute! The very thought of it made his weary bones ache twice as much, for he knew his pockets were empty, and the comforts that lay just beyond those swaying pine trees were far, far from his grasp.

With a moan and a slight shiver — it was getting chilly as the sun sank — Shimon heaved his pack onto his tired back and started plodding along the road again, unrefreshed by his short rest. His mind told him that he had better hurry, but his legs were leaden, and his heart heavier still.

Another mile, and yet another, passed slowly but steadily. At last Shimon actually began to believe that he would soon be back in Zelstadt and his troubles would be over. Memories of his hometown, and especially his visits with the rabbi and his family, flooded back now and lightened his step. He remembered how "Little Shimie," the rabbi's son, always welcomed him especially enthusiastically, for he was the boy's special friend: didn't they share the same name? "Little Shimie" and "Big Shimie," the children had dubbed the pair. The little ones always made him feel like an honored guest, rallying round to hear his reports of Jewish towns and villages they had never seen and had scarcely heard of. Shimon would regale them with tales of his adventures, his bargains, and his profitable deals (and some that were not so profitable, too). The children were always captivated by his stories, and their affection and admiration filled his heart with a warmth he could feel even now.

Without realizing it, Shimon quickened his pace. Tender memories had infused him with new strength. Soon he would be home — just another mile or so!

"Ah," he recalled, "the rabbi and rebbetzin treat me like a prince, with respect and warmth.

True," he mused, "it must be because of my late father, may he rest in peace, the saintly Reb David, who had been the town's beloved *melamed* for years and years."

Shimon rounded a bend and the first houses came into sight. How clearly he recalled the last time he had left Zelstadt to set out on his circuit of peddling.

"Do you have everything, Big Shimie?" Little Shimie had asked solicitously. "Your tallis and tefillin, and your siddur? And the warm scarf my sister Shani knitted for you?"

"Don't forget this," the rebbetzin had said, offering him some carefully wrapped provisions for the way. "You'll be hungry soon enough, trudging along those rough roads with your heavy load."

"Thank you," Shimon mumbled gratefully as he tucked the food into his sack. "You're so good to me!"

Then the rabbi had given him his blessings for the way. Shimon relived the whole scene in his mind. How often he had recalled the rabbi's parting words: "...and remember, if you ever need anything, we're just waiting to help you. We're your family, Shimon, so don't hesitate to let us know if you ever need something. That's what family is for!"

A sigh escaped Shimon's lips when he recalled how sick he had been just two months earlier among strangers. *Baruch Hashem*, they, too, had helped him, but it wasn't the same as in Zelstadt. No one found him work, no one cooked him special meals to help him regain his strength. After all, he was only a stranger. How could he expect them to do more than get him up and around again?

Another sigh shook his soul. He had left Zelstadt half a year ago hale and hearty, and now he was returning home a hunched-over, white-haired old man. He hardly recognized himself as "Big Shimie," who had frolicked with the children and always had a smile and a kind word for them.

Shimon reached the first houses in the village and trod onward down the main street. Delicious aromas of cooking wafted his way and drew him out of his reverie and back to the reality of his very empty stomach.

Just another block...he was almost running now, despite himself. Here it was — the rabbi's door. He knocked twice and could just picture the children's delight when they laid eyes on him. Little Shimie must have grown; would he mind being called "*Little*" Shimie?

Someone was coming to open the door...the rabbi himself! Shimon didn't say a word; he just waited for the rabbi to welcome him into the house and call the others to enjoy the surprise.

But it didn't happen. The rabbi stood there a moment, looking at Shimon as though he were a total stranger. Seeing that Shimon said nothing, he asked, "Yes? May we help you with something, Reb Yid? You're a newcomer to our town, aren't you?"

Shimon was too shocked for words. A newcomer? To Zelstadt? To this house? To the only home he could lay any sort of claim to? What had happened? What had gone wrong? What had he done?

"I, I..." he stammered, but the words didn't come.

The two men stood there in the doorway, the rabbi being as kind, patient, reserved, and dignified as he would be with any stranger. Shimon also waited...but for what? What could he expect of strangers? But were these *strangers*? His head was spinning.

"Tatte, Tatte, who's there? Who came to us?" a child's voice reached Shimon's ears. A sweet-faced boy of ten, eyes wide with curiosity and *peiyos* swinging to and fro, peeped out from behind the rabbi.

Little Shimie! Shimon's heart leapt. Surely *he* would remember his namesake.

"*Shalom aleichem*, Little Shimie!" Shimon managed to half-whisper, reaching out to pinch the lad's cheek. But Shimie was too old to let a mere stranger touch him; in a flash, he turned and fled back into the house. Little Shimie, his beloved Little Shimie, hadn't recognized him.

It was the final blow for Shimon; he collapsed on the steps in a fit of sobs: "There's no hope for me; I'm finished! Even my closest friends don't know me anymore!"

Hashem promised *bnei Yisrael* that no misfortune would ever befall them for more than three days, as the prophet Hoshea says: "After two days He will revive us, [and] on the third day He will raise us up, and we shall live before Him" (Hoshea 6:2).

Indeed, in the time of Mordechai and Esther, the people fasted three days and their evil decree was averted. The conniving Haman was hanged, and his estate transferred to Mordechai — after three days of sincere repentance and prayer to Hashem.

Today, however, it is difficult to understand the words of Hoshea. One calamity after another strikes our people for months or even years. World War II lasted more than five years. Communism plagued the Jewish people and suffocated the flames of Torah and mitzvos for over seventy years. What happened? Surely Hashem had the power to save us sooner, had He wanted to; but for some reason, He chose to prolong our suffering despite the words of the *navi.* Why?

The Dubno Maggid explains that when Jews gather together to pray for mercy, their tears and pleas arouse our forefathers Avraham, Yitzchak, and Yaakov to beg Hashem to take pity on their children, *Am Yisrael,* and save them. In the merit of the holy *Avos,* who served Hashem faithfully in test after test, we, their children's children, are spared tragedy and anguish.

But this applies only when our actions clearly show that we are the children of Avraham, Yitzchak, and Yaakov. For instance, what distinguishes Avraham's descendants from the other nations of the world? Chazal write that anyone who has pity on his fellow man is clearly a descendant of Avraham Avinu (*Yevamos* 79a). Therefore, any generation that does not excel in *chesed,* in acts of kindness and charity, does not deserve the title of "children of Avraham Avinu." Even their loving father, who had pleaded their cause fervently before the Throne of Glory, no longer recognizes them as his own children, and consequently no longer prays for them.

Our job is to prove ourselves worthy children

of the *Avos*, to earn the right to benefit from their special merit in the eyes of Hashem. Do our actions clearly show that we are different? Is our heritage, our holy lineage, evident to all? We must guard against the tendency to become more and more like those around us. We must strive tirelessly to preserve our identity as the heirs of the holy founders of our nation. Only then will we be worthy of "...He will raise us up, and we shall live before Him."

Behar-Bechukosai
Placing the Blame

אִם בְּחֻקֹּתַי תֵּלֵכוּ וְאֶת מִצְוֹתַי תִּשְׁמְרוּ וַעֲשִׂיתֶם אוֹתָם.

If you walk in My laws, and keep My commandments, and fulfill them....
(Vayikra 26:3-4)

The next eight verses describe all the blessings Hashem will grant us when we keep His mitzvos faithfully: There will be more food than we need. We'll have no fear of wild beasts, or other disasters. We will easily vanquish our enemies. And we'll become a numerous, powerful nation in which Hashem's Presence is felt by all.

On the other hand, the Torah continues, if *chas vechalilah,* we leave the path of mitzvos, one misfortune after another will befall the Jewish people.

In explaining these verses, the Midrash quotes a verse from Hoshea (14:10): "...for the paths of Hashem are straight. The righteous will walk along them, but those who sin will stumble upon them."

If the paths of Hashem are straight, why do sinners stumble upon them? The Dubno Maggid explains with a *mashal*:

The Tamarisk Inn was well-known for miles around, not only for the tempting meals Reb Avraham and his wife served, but for the warm, sunny welcome that every guest, rich or poor, received.

"A bit more soup, Reb David? How about another helping of stew, Reb Gershon?" Reb Avraham generously offered the town's two beggars second portions as though they were aristocratic guests. "Anything else I can bring you, *rabbosai*?"

"Thank you, Reb Avraham. Its all delicious! A whiff of *olam haba*! I think I will have another plate of stew, if you don't mind. It's just too tasty to turn down," replied Reb David, whose ample figure testified to his hearty appetite.

There were no leftovers at the Tamarisk when Reb David was at the table. Reb Avraham always urged him not to be shy, but this time Reb Gershon tried to limit his friend's second and third helpings:

"You know what the doctor told you last week. It's heavy meals that are giving you those painful liver attacks. You've got no choice. You'll just have to eat less if you don't want to end up in bed again, moaning for hours until your aches and pains finally go away. Remember, he also said that you can cause permanent damage to your liver, *chas vechalilah,* if you're not careful. Why take the risk? You know better than anyone else how much it hurts afterwards."

"Oh, come on, Reb Gershon. I'm taking just a bit," retorted Reb David defensively as he scooped the juicy chunks of beef and vegetables onto his plate.

Reb Gershon had to admit that it was a smallish portion — compared to the first two helpings Reb David had already downed with such relish.

Reb Avraham was worried at the news of the doctor's warning. "Please do look after yourself, Reb David. I would be so upset if you became ill after a meal here at the Tamarisk!"

"Don't worry about me, Reb Avraham. You know I've been enjoying your meals for years, and no one ever claimed I didn't do justice to your kind wife's cooking. Look at me: Healthy as a horse, no? Picture of health, *baruch Hashem.* If you're going to be concerned about anyone, it should be Reb Gershon. He's always indulging in 'just another sip' of some vintage wine or other, until he's so completely drunk that he makes a fool of himself in front of the whole town."

"Come to think of it," Reb Gershon cut in before Reb Avraham could reply, "a superb meal like this one *does* deserve a hearty *lechaim.* Don't you agree, Reb Avraham?"

"Help yourselves, *rabbosai*," answered Reb Avraham gently as he passed a well-filled flask around the table. "But please, my friends, don't overdo it. Look after your health. You both know better than anyone else what is good for you and what isn't."

"Ah, the Tamarisk's specialty — red burgundy!" exclaimed Reb Gershon with obvious delight as he filled every glass in sight, including, of course, his own. One glass led to another, and soon, Reb Gershon was as full of burgundy as his friend Reb David was of beef stew and dumplings.

A warm, friendly atmosphere reigned at the Tamarisk as the last of the guests finished their sumptuous meals and retired to easy chairs in front of the fireplace to exchange the latest bits of news in the glow of the flames. Stomachs full, minds at ease, everyone seemed relaxed and content.

But an hour or so later, the scene changed abruptly. Reb David, lulled to sleep by his rich, heavy meal and the cozy warmth, suddenly awoke screaming in pain: "Help me!"

Too startled to know where he was, or whether it was day or night, Reb David knew only one thing: his liver hurt! The mixture of bewilderment, fright, and anguish on his face made it clear to all that this was no passing nightmare. Reb David was very much awake, and his pains — and screams — were very real.

"Help! A doctor! Help me! I'm dying!"

Writhing in pain, Reb David slid off his armchair and onto the wooden floor before his startled companions could catch him. Reb Avraham came running into the room and was the first to kneel over the patient.

"Shmuel! Gershon! Quickly! Fetch Dr. Greenhaus! Fast!"

Shmuel was out the door in a flash, but Gershon wasn't even aware of his friend's plight. The burgundy had done its work: The only sign of life from the corner that sheltered the soundly sleeping Gershon was the occasional rupture of a loud, drunken snore.

But right now, all eyes were focused on the center of the room, where Reb Avraham was trying in vain to ease Reb David's pain.

"Reb Avraham," moaned David, his eyes fluttering open and closed with pain, "what did you feed me? What was in that stew? Was the meat bad? Or was it the soup. Maybe it was left over from Shabbos? Ohhhh," he moaned, rolling to one side. "What did you do to me, Reb Avraham? Ohhhh...."

"Reb David! How can you imagine that I, of all people, would want to hurt you? Why should I want to see you suffer? Here I have tried for years to look after you, and feed you the best foods when you were hungry, and give you a warm, comfortable bed when you had nowhere to go.

"Look," Reb Avraham tried to reason with Reb David, "everyone in this room had the same stew, the same soup, the same dumplings as you just did. They're all healthy, *baruch Hashem.* They all feel fine. It's only you who is suffering like this. There must be something wrong with you, not with the food."

The other guests at the inn were aghast at Reb David's brazen accusations. For years Reb Avraham had cared for Reb David, and now he was blaming him for having given him a delicious free meal!

"Fool! What an ungrateful fool!" roared the guests at the moaning Reb David. "How can you accuse a tzaddik like Reb Avraham of wanting to harm you when he has bent over backwards to help you? You know the doctor warned you not to eat so much, and especially not such heavy, rich foods. You went right ahead and poisoned yourself — even though Reb Gershon warned you not to. And now you have the chutzpah to go and blame a tzaddik like Reb Avraham, who has fed you and looked after you as only a father and a brother would! Haven't you a grain of gratitude in you? You've got no one to blame but yourself!"

Just then, Shmuel returned with Dr. Greenhaus, and with what seemed like half the town on their heels. The doctor ordered several hefty villagers to carry Reb David off to a side room. Then he and Reb Avraham disappeared behind the closed door.

The rest of the crowd remained in the large sitting room, recounting how Reb Avraham had done so much *chesed* for Reb David, and how even now he was in there caring for him. Who was going to pay the doctor's bill, buy the medicines, and wait on Reb David hand and foot until he recovered? Who if not Reb Avraham, the tzaddik?

The men milled around the room, retelling and rehashing the events of the day, first with one friend, then with another. In all the commotion, someone stumbled over the still-sleeping Reb Gershon, whose snoring had been drowned out by all the voices. Awakened suddenly, he tried to jump to his feet but his head was reeling. The walls seemed to be shaking to and fro as he struggled to maintain his balance, and he was sure the floorboards were teetering up and down beneath him.

"An earthquake! Run! Run for your lives!" he shouted hoarsely, trying to get his rubbery legs to propel him to the door. One hand on his spinning head, the other on whatever support he could find, Reb Gershon stumbled around the room while, one after another, the villagers fell silent and stared at the new spectacle unfolding right before their eyes. Reb Gershon was truly convinced that the inn was about to collapse — heaven forbid — and bury them all on the spot.

"It's not the earth that's shaking, Reb Gershon; it's your legs. All that wine has gone to your head — that's what's wobbling. The earth is as steady as ever, *baruch Hashem!*"

"Steady?" asked Reb Gershon thickly. "Just take a look at those walls swaying back and forth. And if there isn't an earthquake, why can't I walk straight to the door?"

"Look, Reb Gershon, *I* can make a beeline for the door. No problem," said Yitzchak, striding snappily towards the front door.

"Me, too," followed Shimshon.

"So can we," chimed in Ezra, grabbing Shlomo's arm and marching him off in Shimshon's direction.

"You're just drunk, Reb Gershon. It's not the walls and the floor that are shaky, it's your own head that's full of wine!"

If only the gluttonous Reb David and the drunken Reb Gershon had recognized their faults and corrected them, they could have walked smoothly along the path of life.

But instead, they blamed their difficulties on the path itself, be it the helping hand of Reb Avraham or the solid ground beneath Reb Gershon's feet. Consequently, they stumbled.

Likewise, we must not blame our misfortune on Hashem. For His paths are straight — it's just a question of whether we choose to walk along them, keeping to the path, and following in His Ways, as the *pasuk* says: "If you walk in My laws, and keep My commandments, and fulfill them...."